Bad Imaginings

BAD IMAGININGS

CAROLINE ADDERSON

The Porcupine's Quill, Inc.

CANADIAN CATALOGUING IN PUBLICATION DATA

Adderson, Caroline, 1963-
Bad imaginings

ISBN 0-88984-172-1

I. Title.

PS8551.D34B3 1993   C813'.54   C93-095098-4
PR9199.3.A33B3 1993

Published by The Porcupine's Quill, Inc., 68 Main Street, Erin, Ontario NOB 1TO with financial assistance from The Canada Council and the Ontario Arts Council. The support of the Government of Ontario through the Ministry of Culture, Tourism and Recreation is also gratefully acknowledged.

Distributed by General Distribution Services Inc., 34 Lesmill Road, Don Mills, Ontario M3B 2T6.

Readied for the press by John Metcalf.
Copy edited by Doris Cowan.

Cover is after the painting 'Martha Bartlett with her Kitten', American, artist unknown. Copyright © 1981 by The Metropolitan Museum of Art, N.Y.C.

Typeset in Trump Mediaeval, printed and bound by the Porcupine's Quill. The stock is acid-free Zephyr Antique Laid.

Second printing, February 1994.

For my mother, father and sister

*

I am grateful for the faith, encouragement and advice offered by so many. In particular, I would like to thank Kathy Garneau, John Metcalf, Morna McLeod, Don Coles, Steven Heighton and my very good friends from the Banff Centre for the Arts 1991 Studios. I am also indebted to the late Adele Wiseman.

For their financial support, I would like to thank the Canada Council, The Canada Council Explorations Program, Alberta Culture and the Ontario Arts Council.

CONTENTS

SHINERS

LAURENCE IS WADING stiff-legged into the lake, plastic bucket in one hand, the other reassuring the top of his head. Their grandmother has got him to put on a little sailor cap. Blue trunks, Thad's of two years before, sag at the crotch. On his chest are raw pink marks, a tender mottling where scabs were peeled off too soon.

Sun-warmed shallows show minnows. Like the blades of small new knives, they are painfully silver, alluring. A cluster hovers over grey-green pebbles. The water is knee-deep to Thad, thigh-deep to Laurence.

Thad says, 'Give me the bucket.' Poised, he bends low, careful that his shadow does not cross the fishes and disperse them or, blocking light, unsilver them so they disappear. He is feeling for the best moment to strike. Then Laurence, sucking in his breath, causes Thad to start. His movement disturbs the water, sends out ripples that counter the waves and make a tiny liquid jarring. The minnows flick across the rocks, the yellow sand bottom of the lake, and away.

'Little shit,' Thad hisses.

'I didn't do anything!' says Laurence.

'You breathed!'

Laurence pulls the sailor cap over his eyes. He groans. Throwing down the pail, Thad leaves the water to lie on the sand. Laurence comes and stands over him. 'I didn't do anything. Tha-ad? Or are you just mad again because you failed?'

This question is without malice, Thad knows, but it's of little consolation. He opens one terrible eye and Laurence cowers. Even before Thad moves, Laurence begins running down the beach, arms flailing. This is why he runs so slowly, Thad thinks. Not because he has a plastic thing in his heart, but because his arms move faster than his legs and through so much air, so inefficiently. Thad lets him go a distance, then leaps, sprints, catches Laurence by the swimming trunks, yanks him to the ground, pushes his face in the sand, grinds it there. Laurence sits up spitting sand out of his mouth. There is a circle of red around one nostril.

'You big shit.' He tilts back his head and pinches his nose. He never cries.

Thad says nothing. He begins, though, chewing on his bottom lip, the way he does when he is sorry. When he has been unkind. He has failed at school, failed grade six because he watches too much television someone said. Probably the teacher. What he misses most are the Saturday morning cartoons.

Their grandmother calls from the cabin. Thad helps Laurence to his feet, replaces the cap and walks with his arm around his brother.

She is watching the boys, the little one scurrying like a distressed insect, Thad so big and hale. She doesn't much like children, yet these grandchildren keep coming around. Thad is okay; she has a soft spot for the bad ones who can never get it right. Laurence, sick in the heart from birth, is treated too much like a holy thing and she can't believe it hasn't gone to his head. The girls, though, are the worst with their plastic radios, flip-flop sandals and flowery beach towels, always hysterical over spiders.

She was never interested in children, yet her whole life has been kissing bloodied knees, reciting idiot rhymes, giving care. It's perfunctory second nature now. At thirteen she was plucked from school to mother her sisters. She remembers herself in bare feet and a hand-me-down cardigan, they were that poor. The three little girls playing with a feather boa that came off a relief train. At seventeen she was working as a domestic for an engineer and his wife. She used to bring their children around to Nathan's flat and leave them with a Ukrainian downstairs who could play the accordion. While she and Nathan made love on his sofa they heard through the floorboards the wheezing of Old World melodies and the accordion became for them, half in jest, the most erotic of instruments. She didn't worry about the children finking because one was retarded and the other she could pinch and slap into submission and, anyway, the engineer was in love and wouldn't say boo to her.

Then looking after her own child, living with her mother and sister, suffering their self-righteousness. Nathan was in the army stationed abroad, so she wore her mother's wedding ring. Dependence, constant petty bickering, it was the worst time for her and as a consequence she could never love her first child. Undernourished and colicky, he repelled her. Now, almost fifty, he wrote her a letter telling of breakdowns and divorces, saying he is unable to feel loved in his relationships, asking once and for all what she had against him. She felt sorry for him and wrote back that he was her precious treasure, when in reality he is the personification of all her woes and frustrations. She had five more children by Nathan and now has eight grandchildren.

The cabin is just beyond the beach and a narrow spread of wild grass, sitting in the shadow of pines. Crossing the grass, both boys are watchful for snakes. They are hopeful snake-catchers. Sometimes Thad turns over the stones on the path for this purpose, exasperating their grandmother because he never replaces them. They talk of pythons and boa constrictors, anacondas, but will gladly settle for less.

Carlyle, their Labrador gone blind, lies in the doorway. Thad gives one of the ears, worn and tatty as an old flag, a sharp tug. Grunting, the dog swings its head frantically, staring out of silvering eyes.

'Are you teasing again?' She stands on the other side of the screen door, a thick-middled figure in a cotton dress, white braid hanging over her shoulder. There is a cragginess in her voice that could be anger, but is really age and fatigue.

'You saw me, didn't you!'

'Shhh.' She makes the sound of dry leaves on concrete, of light rain, to let him know she was not accusing. He is so touchy. She smiles. She still has her own teeth, scary teeth Laurence says, one broken off diagonally. Shaking her head, she opens the door, handing them their T-shirts as they file past.

Although the summer days draw out, long as a skein of bargain twine, light until eleven o'clock, the cabin, in the enclave of tall pines, the circle of continual scent and shadow, is always dark. There are electric lights but because they attract insects – great clumsy bat-winged moths, mosquitoes – their grandmother rarely uses them. Instead they have oil lamps; the boys like these better anyway.

Laurence and Thad sit opposite one another at the table. She sets before each of them an enamel dish of beans, a wiener sliced across the top. There is a story about these metal dishes, that they were given to their grandmother after their grandfather's stroke when she hurled her every piece of china against the side of the cabin. It is a story Laurence does not believe; Thad fancies she threw them at their grandfather and that is why he had a stroke.

Thad grimaces at the food. She laughs and feels Laurence's forehead, asks, 'Good day?'

'Good day!' says Laurence, full of beans.

When she goes for the lamp, Thad bends back his spoon and catapults a piece of wiener at his brother.

'We're going to get the eggs after supper,' she says, setting the lamp on the table. She touches a match to the wick. The flame springs and shadows slip into the room, flattening themselves around the walls.

'Do I have to go?' asks Thad. There is a girl Thad's age at the farm where they buy eggs. She wears her hair cropped and a halter top through which he can detect two soft cones of flesh. Last week she called him a lunkhead. 'I won't go.'

After supper they step behind the Chinese screen that separates their sleeping area from the kitchen and pull jeans over their now-dry swimming trunks. Their grandmother is in the bedroom setting up the tray for their grandfather. This visit the boys have seldom looked in on their grandfather. Not a pretty sight like he used to be, their grandmother says. The boys go out and sit on the beach and wait for her.

'What are you thinking about?' asks Laurence.

'Rocky and Bullwinkle.' He traces a snaky mark in the sand with his foot, then points over the water. 'Look. Do you see it?'

'What?'

'There. A canoe.'

Laurence stands and, shading his eyes, studies the imaginary line where water wets sky.

'Are you blind?' says Thad.

'There isn't any canoe!' Laurence cries.

She feeds him less than gently, spoon scraping across naked gums. When she met him he was lathing broom handles in a factory and his forearms and wrists were so large he could not close the cuffs on his shirt. That was 1935 and no other man has interested her since. Such a beautiful skull and hair she could grab in both hands and still not catch half of. Even in old age, before his stroke, she never lost physical desire for him.

When his job closed and he went on relief she would give him her liquor rations and bring fruit and chocolate from the engineer's house. Then the war broke out and they were separated for two terrible years while she, knowing he would not be faithful, prayed that at least he would not marry overseas. He did return, but because he had run away from the army, they came up north just like fugitives and nearly starved the first winter, she pregnant again. Nathan began running fishing expeditions on the lake and they built two cabins. One day he had a vacationing police constable as a client.

The years Nathan spent in prison, she worked in a garment factory to support their three children. When he was released in 1950, they were finally able to marry. They spent their honeymoon night back in their cabin quarrelling through the tense climax of realized dreams. He hit her in the face, breaking her tooth. It did not dim her happiness; such struggle was part of love. She was always proud of his strong body and his force, his good looks.

She wipes the flaccid face with the bib, then feels around under the quilt, checking padded pants for moisture.

In the station wagon, Thad climbs over the seat to the very back and lies beside the spare tire among the clutter of egg trays and flower pots and old newspapers. Laurence sits in front with their grandmother.

'We're going to have a storm,' she says. 'Look at that sky.'

Thad presses his face against the glass and sees the thickening grey. The tree stands they pass are completely still. He almost expects to hear Laurence suck in his breath from the tension. When they pull into the farm, it appears deserted, the animals gone away to wait out the rain.

Their grandmother takes an egg tray from the back as the brothers clamber out of the car, slamming doors. She gives it to Thad and he and Laurence go to fetch the eggs while she rings at the house.

The egg shed is for washing and storing. It stinks of chicken dirt and mouldy feed. They enter, Laurence plugging his nose, and the girl is standing with her back to them, bending over the sink. She wears denim cut-offs and that halter-top, the frayed ties double-knotted against boys. Her sneakers and bare legs are muddied.

'Heggs please,' says Laurence, still plugging his nose.

She turns and looks at Laurence, her expression softly curious, and Thad realizes she knows something about them. She sees him.

'Lunkhead.'

He reddens, but cannot think of a suitable reply.

'If you want heggs, you can wash them yourself,' she tells Laurence, feigning contempt and holding out the brush. He grins. Last week she let him wash too.

Laurence talks to the girl as he cleans the eggs under the dribble of tap water. Thad stands behind with the tray and she loads.

'We almost caught these shiners today.' He hesitates. 'Thad almost caught them.'

'What's a shiner?'

'A small fish. A – '

'Punch in the eye,' says Thad.

She glances at him. She has blue eyes and in the left one,

under the pupil, a spot of yellow. Seeing it, he immediately lowers his gaze to the bib of her halter top.

'Then I sneezed or something. Anyway, we didn't catch them after all.'

'Too bad.'

'Yeah. Thad got mad.'

'Lunkhead,' she says.

Thad reddens again. Then it occurs to him she just might know he has failed a grade. He drops the tray and shouts at Laurence.

'Why don't you shut up? Why don't you go straight to hell?'

There is a long silence. He has never said go to hell in his life. It is something he heard on television.

The girl will not look at him. She pats Laurence on the head. 'It's okay. You two clean that up and I'll wash the eggs.'

At Thad's feet, the yolks are the same colour as that spot in her eye.

In no time they are walking silently up to the house, Thad biting hard into his lip. She puts the tray on the hood of the car and they go to sit on the steps. Their grandmother is standing in the parlour with the woman who owns the farm. She is a widow and the mother of the girl, Thad remembers. He can hear them now through the screen door, talking about Laurence.

'Born that way,' their grandmother says. 'This year he had an operation.'

'And now?'

'He's fine, thanks be to God. They put a rubber ball or garden hose or some such thing in his heart. Be right as rain soon. Now it's the elder boy we worry about. Thad was shaken up bad.'

'Because of his brother being sick?'

'You know how children blame themselves. Anyway, he had trouble at school and whatnot. Bad imaginings.'

The other woman clicks her tongue softly. 'He thought he was going to lose his brother.'

'Oh, the temper! I see it like this,' says their grandmother. 'Love on account of fear is a difficult thing to manage. It wells up and gets kind of desperate. Don't we know about that? Watching husbands go?'

On the step, Laurence promises a snake. 'But don't blame me!'

'For what?'

'If it steals an egg and swallows it whole!'

Driving back, all of them in the front seat, it begins to rain. Only one windshield wiper works so the brothers watch the road through blear and smear. Presently the horizon lights up in sheets, then fades, lights again, this time cut through by brilliant jags.

The worst thing about a storm is that they must stay inside. Laurence, used to long hours of solitude, hunches over the table reading a *Scamp* comic. Their grandmother washes dishes. Thad does not usually read, so he paces. Every time he passes Carlyle lying behind the telephone stand, the dog growls.

'Old shit,' says Thad and he slips into the bedroom and stands staring at his grandfather.

The old man sits in a wing-backed armchair beside the bed. A patchwork quilt is tucked around his legs, his obvious knees like the bulbs of those glass telephone wire insulators on the shelf above the sink. Though the body is aged, the face, perhaps from swelling, seems young and unlined. His eyes are a clear grey, milky hair a fringe around his glowing head. His mouth hangs slack and a line of spittle crosses his chin, darkens his breast. Laurence is there now standing next to Thad.

On the table by their grandfather is a bowl of mints, clear like ice. Thad crosses the room and takes a candy, unwraps and pops it in his mouth, sits on the bed. He throws one to Laurence who misses and must feel around for it under the bureau.

Thad cocks his ear toward their grandfather. 'What? Speak up! You want one too, Grandpa?' He grins at Laurence.

Laurence comes and takes a candy, stands there holding it, staring at the floor. Thad giggles.

'What?' asks Laurence, smiling. 'What's so funny?'

Soon they are both on the bed, holding their bellies,

directing their laughter into the bedspread. Neither can identify the source of this mirth; it is just one of those moments between brothers. Then Laurence sits up and puts the wrapped candy in their grandfather's mouth. Immediately he begins sucking, an innocent look of surprise on his face like an infant not expecting the nipple. The tail of cellophane between his lips turns around and around.

'Do it again!' says Thad.

It is too funny, the way the old man puckers his lips like a fish, how he tongues a second candy, gentle greed. Even when he coughs, the wrappers tickling, the brothers are stifling each other's laughter with their clowning hands.

They hear the telephone ring and tear out of the room.

'Yes, they're fine,' says their grandmother. 'Here they are now. Here's Laurie.'

He grabs the receiver and begins babbling. 'Shiners! Don't you know what shiners are? Mom! They're minnows! You really didn't know?'

Thad takes the phone and she asks him how he is doing without a television. He says he has not even noticed.

After they hang up, their grandmother herds them into the kitchen for washing, then lets them pee from the door stoop. There is a bathroom but that is not as much fun. She takes an oil lamp and sets it on the table behind the Chinese screen so the boys can chat before going to sleep. She lays her hand across Laurence's forehead, then kisses them both. Coming through the wall so faintly is the sound of their grandfather coughing. They strip off their jeans and т-shirts and pile onto the bed, still in trunks.

'I want that side,' says Laurence, meaning the side next to the table so he'll be the one to put out the lamp.

'No way,' says Thad.

'Big shit,' says Laurence feebly.

Thad cuffs him on the head. 'Little shit.'

In the bedroom their grandfather coughs raggedly, persistently. They hear their grandmother's voice too, softly first, then rising to alarm.

Suddenly the overhead light is on. The boys have not seen

electric light for almost two weeks and it pains and startles. She is standing over them, her hair loose and her dress half-unbuttoned. They have never known her angry and this is fury. She shakes a clotted scrap of cellophane in Thad's face.

'He was choking!'

'Laurie did it!' Thad blurts, then takes his bottom lip between his teeth.

Laurence stares animal-faced.

'Did you?'

'Yes.'

Leaning over Thad, she grabs Laurence by the arm. She shakes him out wildly, as if his badness is dust.

'My man, big man,' she sighs, drawing his limp arm out of the sleeve, running her hands over the angles of his bones. She is naked herself, gnarly bare toes on the cold wood floor, breasts sloping to rest on the shelf of her belly. She leans into him, ear-to-ear, slides her hands under his buttocks and this way can lift him from chair to bed. The plastic undersheet crackles like fire as she lays him out long. He is staring loose-mouthed at the ceiling. She climbs into bed and lowers herself carefully on top of him, spreads her big thighs around the bracket of his jutting hips, rests her elbows by his shoulders and bends to kiss his face, his unresisting mouth. 'Big man.' There is no tuneful respiration of an accordion, just the rain outside rushing against the roof in wind-sent waves and the chimes that hang in the pine boughs clanging like cymbals.

The boys lie in shocked silence staring at the ceiling beams, the hillscape shadow of their profiles on the cabin wall. Somehow a moth has made its haphazard way into the cabin and it drives itself stupidly against the lamp. Thudding, thudding. In the bedroom, their grandmother is murmuring.

Laurence sits up and, clutching fearfully at his own legs, begins to cry. Not aloud, that is not his way, though neither is crying. He just sits there staring, his face twisted, tears and mucus flowing.

'I did a mean thing!'

'Shut up,' whispers Thad. He gnaws his lip.

'I did such a mean thing to Grandpa!'

'Shut up, please!'

Laurence, face in hands, falls into the pillows. Spasming grief, he clenches and unclenches his body. It seems like hours Thad must suffer Laurence's quivering, hear his cloggy, gasping breath until it finally rises to a snore twice the size of him.

Then Thad is alone in the discordant night – wind chimes clashing, their grandmother murmuring, the moth's monotonous self-battering. He touches his finger to his lip and stares at it. He is bleeding.

GOLD MOUNTAIN
(A TALE OF FORTUNE-SEEKING IN
BRITISH NORTH AMERICA)

Showing in brief my present Straits and their pitiful Origin

NOW I AM a remittance man of the worst kind, the unwitting kind who leaves home expressly to support his needy, but ends up gnawing on their empty outstretched hands. Example: in England my poor mother, before opening my letters, will shake them, listening vainly for a coin-like jangle. Finding instead more beggarly words, she rebukes me by return post. Financial insecurity distresses her digestion. When my father was alive and providing amply, she never so much as broke wind.

My father owned a shoe shop in Salisbury where he dressed men's feet as a priest might souls. His passion for the vamp, the heel and upper I inherited, though not his knack at turning pennies. For sums I have no nerve. Thus my widowed mother's suggestion that I come to the colonies where I might practise a simpler commerce, man-to-man from the back of a horse, my breast pocket for a bank.

Landing in Montreal, I was brash and optimistic. My mercantile scheme I had bolstered with a loftier ideal: the civilizing influence of fine footwear. I heard a wretched plea from deep in the wilderness and so, as the missionary goes bearing The Word to the isolated and deprived, I went to the barefoot and clodhoppered with Bluchers and Balmorals. A season later, having crossed the maddening plains, I had become a ragged peripatetic, my neck scabbed with horsefly bites, a fungal garden growing on my tongue. How in good conscience could I continue thrusting the corns and calluses of peasants into the shoe of lords? I flung my peddler's case into the river and, though never wont to indulge in spirits, vowed to finish my days in the Dominion of Failure on a saloon stool, marinating myself in brandy, then, like a Christmas pudding, setting myself aflame.

That saloon was here in Everlasting, this frontier town, these hundred meanly-shod inhabitants. Everlasting. Try to find it on your map.

In which, cajoled by Drink, I seal my Fate as a Gold-Seeker

I AM A SLIGHT MAN, two inches and five feet in stacked heels – a near match for the slumbering dog I met in the saloon doorway. Recalling a certain wise old adage, I hastened to retreat. Just then a voice from inside the saloon hailed me.

'Step on over 'im! He's more an angel than a hound!'

The cur's owner proved to be Mr Bernard Coop. (The day before, ignoring that he wore no collar, that his flies were spotty and partially unbuttoned, I had tried to sell him a truly resplendent pair of Balmorals, the self-same pair now on its way to sea.) He bade me take a seat, then bought a quantum of brandy that plied my shameless tongue. Before long I had disclosed the trouble with my mother's digestion. 'Selling dancing slippers never made a body rich,' snorted Coop. 'All the smart ones are going to Cariboo for staking claims.'

Coop had a scheme which he outlined thus: assemble a party of rude young men and lead them into Cariboo. Give them tents and meals and wages for their placer mining. The gold itself, keep yourself – at a handsome profit. Coop was to be the overseer. He was looking for someone to recruit the men and keep the camp tidy. I being, in Coop's words, 'runty and very spruce' was just the man. Did I agree?

'Where is Cariboo?' I enquired.

'I've no hell idea.'

He refilled my glass, then held his own out to make a toast. There I sat, penniless, my livelihood bobbing down a river – a beggar, not a chooser. Reluctantly I too raised my glass. We drank and afterward, to doubly seal our fate, shook hands. I recoiled. Where on his right hand his middle fingers should have been, were two unsightly stumps. 'At least the good one's left, Mr Merritt,' he said, wagging the finger at me, then, with it, reaming out his ear.

How, in a clean and starched Shirt Front, I am truly smitten

A DECENT CHANGE of boots (capped toes, four gay buttons) was still in my possession, but for clothes I had only those clinging to my back. Needs were, I hired myself a laundress, a sympathetic lady who let me wait undraped in her parlour while the wash water evaporated from my shirt tails. 'Funny. I'm not a bit ashamed,' she confessed. 'You seem more a lady than a fellow. What's your trade?'

'I ease and beautify mankind's weary tread.'

'A cobbler?'

'A peddler, alas. But I hope now to try my luck at gold.' Then I told her of Coop's and my plan for Cariboo, could we ever find the place.

'My cousin Evaline is a cartographer.'

'A lady cartographer?'

'Of sorts.'

'Of sorts a lady or of sorts a cartographer?' I jested.

'Both.' She hesitated a moment, then divulged to me the rare nature of her cousin's craft. With her head on her pillow here in Everlasting, Miss Evaline could find me Cariboo. She could find it in her dreams.

When my garments were dried and pressed, my laundress buttoned me. 'Go and see her,' she said.

I had thought a cartographer who dreamed her maps and mapped her dreams would be as airily constructed as an angel. Miss Evaline was a giantess. (Anvil-footed in derby boots, a torso like a stove.) I found her in her barn, arm to her elbow in the backside of a horse. Her mare was late to foal, she bashfully explained, wiping on her skirt the equine slime. 'She'll drop before the stars come out. Upon my word.'

Then she invited me to tea and in our brief amble to the house I recognized her considerable manly talents. Already demonstrated were her gifts in husbandry. Now I learned that both her barn and house were built by her person alone. Further, she was sole master of this range, a full one hundred and sixty acres.

In her parlour she poured me a cup of mire, then proffered on a washboard her stony biscuits. I cast a glance around – at hides and burlap sacks, sundry implements, unpapered walls. Espying a rack of scrolls, I asked, 'Are those your maps?'

She rose to fetch one and together we unfurled it.

'It's just a pastime.'

'On the contrary,' I declared. 'It's a gift!' Here was a sheet of snow-white parchment. Only close inspection revealed minutiae rendered, not in line, but subtle iridescent shading. Any skills she lacked in pure cartography were made up for in artistry. I saw rills and drifts and locked-in floes. It was indeed snow white; it was snow.

'The North Pole,' she said.

'But it's undiscovered!'

'If it were discovered, I would have drawn a flag.'

Then she showed me the Hawaiian Islands – volcanoes and pineapple plantations – and in New England the terrible charred place where a witch had been burned.

My astonished accolades I could not restrain. Abashed, Miss Evaline set aside the maps and asked if I cared to promenade. At first I mistook her, thinking she meant a dance. 'Walk my range,' she tittered, all afluster, her big hand covering her face. I helped tie her bonnet strings, for she was trembling with shyness, though once we got out walking she grew braver. She took my arm. I took two steps to her every one. 'I have a goodly herd,' she said, so we clambered up a grassy butte and viewed them grazing in the distance. Below us was a sere creek bed, lacy as the bas-relief of a fossil fern. Small clouds cast clear shadows on the flatland. I wondered if in those shapes she read countries.

When we returned to the house, the foal, unborn that morning, was standing in the yard on wavering legs. I was struck then by the marvellous workings of a mere handful of hours. What had not previously existed came into being –

ineffably, delightfully! Then, as if it heard and liked my thought, the foal twitched with joy.

Miss Evaline agreed to help me, though she said it was nothing she had ever done before. To absorb my dream of Cariboo, she brought me to her bed, and it was nothing I had ever done before. In one eager puff she extinguished both her shyness and the lamp, gathered me in hirsute arms, made fly the dust and straw while I, I lay passive – a virgin maid. Why are women named the weaker sex? In intellect they have always seemed to me superior. And now I knew by experience how a woman's fleshly potency can vanquish a man's heart. A long time I lay listening to her windy snore, for once I fell asleep she travelled on to Cariboo, left me behind – alone in love in Everlasting.

Containing the Account of our Travelling out, its Perils, and the droll Characters that We meet upon the Way

IT TOOK A WEEK to ride into British Columbia, where other men with a different dog might have done it in four days. Coop called his creature Bruin, for that was the size and strength of him. At night Bruin molested me in my bedroll. By day he strayed off course to mangle squirrels. As for Coop, he imbibed continuously, dismounting on the hour and making water. All the while I pined for Evaline. At least I had her map which guided us as well as any star.

Note, too, how we were unaccompanied by rude young men. I had petitioned every lad in Everlasting, many of whom gave me an attentive ear, but upon hearing Coop's name, recoiled. Truly, I regretted Coop's and my handshake, but, severed fingers notwithstanding, it bound me to him.

Perilous alpine passes, frigid streams, the omnipresent fear of bears – all this so taxed me that when we finally reached Frazer's River, I was spent. I begged Coop to let me take some days recovering, but as we were then sharing the trail with a contingent of seasoned miners, he feared they would beat us to the best claims. We pressed on, tagging these rivals like, not one, but three smitten dogs. It was they, though, who finally relented, not granting us leave to pass, but inviting us to join them.

Sympathetic to my enfeebled condition, they offered me their freight wagon in which to convalesce. There I lay dreaming of my darling Evaline. I recalled, as a poem learnt in childhood, every detail of her person: her ropy hands and plenteous thighs, the whorl of whiskers round her paps. Delight a potent medicine, before long I had recovered, refreshed and idealistic, my fortune waiting to be panned. With the gold I found I vowed to fashion my love a ring, a seal ring with which to mark her maps. And the beauty of the land revived me further – fireweed blazing along our trail, new growth shivering on the pines, a pale green aura. The river itself, sunlight coloured gold.

Since neither Coop nor I had panned before, I was greedy for good counsel. For the next part of the journey I rode alongside the two hoariest of the fellows, life-long miners flattered to impart their combined wisdom.

On panning itself, one instructed, 'Dunk yer pan, but not too deep.'

The other resounded this advice. 'By God, not too deep!'

'Flush out the silt, but not too much.'

'By God, not too much!'

To discourage bears sing bawdy ditties, not for the lyrics but the din. Burn green wood to repel flies. They warned me, too, against the villains we might encounter: the travelling pastor, the savage Native and the Gold Commissioner. As for the moon-eyed Chinese, he is the lowest man in the golden economy.

'A scavenger,' they told me. 'Where you see a Celestial, there's only dregs.'

One night, as we sat around a leaping fire, someone took out a violin and began sawing a despondent tune. The clearing – towering columns of trees, vault of branches – might have been the great choirspace of Salisbury. My soul, an even smaller being hunkering down inside me, was greatly soothed. Then one of the men cried, 'How about a dance?' Immediately the dirge became a reel and a bale of calico was thrown down from the freight wagon.

When it hit the ground, the bale burst open to reveal a sampling of ladies' dresses. Some of the men stripped to the waist and began donning this unlikely garb with great anticipation. Indeed, the same hoary fellows whose counsel I had esteemed, were now quarrelling over female frippery. Even Bruin, yelping in indignation, was forced into a petticoat.

'Henry Merritt,' someone addressed me. 'Will you be a lady or a fellow?'

'I'll be neither.'

'You dance or you play the fiddle. Can you fiddle?'

'No, sir.'

'Then you dance.'

And into my arms lunged an obscene partner, Coop himself, straining his calico seams at the waist and oxters. When he took my hand, my fingers mingled with his hideous stumps. Most of that macabre night we jigged and swigged and reeled. One lady pirouetting near the fire was set aflame, but kept on twirling till her very beard was singed. It was a nightmare. I mourned the laws of nature even as I danced.

Relating how We are duped into Making Camp and the shocking Truth about our Neighbours. Also, the low Particulars of a Panner's Life

THE MAP SHOWED we had not reached Cariboo, but where our party halted, men were panning in the river below. One eager miner cried, 'Boys, it must be loaded here!' and a hot discussion followed. Some wanted to make camp and reap this certain bounty, while others held steadfast to the promise of Cariboo. 'Henry Merritt, we are bailing out!' Coop suddenly announced. Astonished, I recalled to him our proper destination only to have torn from my hands the precious map. The other fellows then reached immediate accord – they would remain a band and proceed on to Cariboo. This parting advice they offered: exchange with them our horses for staples of victuals and drink. Then Coop and I, against my timid judgement, descended the wooded slope alone.

Of a sudden the mountains reared around us. Their heads, crowned in red, reminded me of a view at ruddy sunset – the line of stony kings on the face of Salisbury Cathedral. And the river, hailing us with its stately roar, magnified my awe. Kneeling at its edge, I saw the mighty workings of that current, how it had ground down the mountains to liberate the gold. For those clear waters were scintillant with gold, with jade too, green nuggets blinking up at me, wildcats' eyes. I pictured the seal on Evaline's ring carved from that verdant stone, the ring upon her sturdy hand, that hand in mine. Then Coop, having gone to investigate the encampment we had seen from the trail, came racing back, hollering and breaking off my vision.

'Celestials! They are Celestials!'

I gaped at him, for this was the import of his discovery: our journey, having worn down equally my boot soles and my nerves, had now ended in an abandoned claim. With neither transport nor lucre, we were stranded, just as sure as Mr Crusoe.

'This, Mr Coop, is what comes of going off the map!'

Though I knew it would but augment my despair, I went to see for myself our Chinese neighbours. Approaching through the trees, I spotted them – five in number, toiling by the river. Down each bent back hung a plait like the long tail of a bell. My mother dressed her hair thus when convalescing, and Evaline, too, abed. They were ladies then! Five Celestial ladies! But an incongruity left me blinking: each was clad in *trousers*. Baffled, I drew within an earshot so as to determine their sex from their voices, yet such clangorous speech told me only that they might have had, too, the tongues of bells. At last one chanced to turn and I saw a bony face of unmistakable masculinity. Shuddering then at the queerness of these people, I hastened back to Coop.

I found him huddled close to Bruin, dog from master indistinguishable in their despondency. I made a fire and prepared our customary meal: salt pork fried in suet, beans and gruel.

We ate in silence, then Coop, with a percolating sniff, laid his dish down for Bruin to clean. Hitherto in our journey I had not perceived in him an emotion that might signify the presence of a soul. Now, tears glistened on his stubbly countenance. It occurred to me also that our weeks together had made him my familiar, that this mutual predicament at least united us, as did, of course, our race. Reaching out, I patted his mutilated hand.

'We'll make the best of this,' I said.

'They'll cut our throats as we sleep!'

'Bruin will be our guard.'

That night a perturbing contradiction set me tossing in my bedroll: abandoned claims the Celestials were said to work, yet I had seen the river sparkle, an aquatic coffer. The next morn this same enigma spurred me headlong to the water. Seeing the Celestials already labouring in the stream, I stopped short, pressed my pan to my breast and in this solemn pose vowed to do the work of five. Then I squatted and commenced to earn my fortune as per the instructions of my erstwhile mentors – filling the pan and swirling it, using the current to flush out the silt. Accordingly, the pan should then have brimmed with nuggets; it brimmed instead with gravel, the gold having washed away. The whole course I then repeated to the same worthless result. Only after many dogged efforts did I learn the trouble: the gold was not formed in nuggets, but flakes like the scales of an auriferous fish. Soon Coop came down to pan as well. 'It's arse gold,' he said, disgusted. 'We're the arses, Henry Merritt.'

If panning was no good to us, we would try another method. First we endeavoured to cull the flecks directly, but our fingers stiffened hopelessly in that frigid water. More successful was extraction by toothpick; after two days, we were a full teaspoon richer.

In the end, I returned to the old method. Toiling thus, I was one day arrested by a dazzling sight: a gold leviathan gliding through our river shedding as it went the glinting scales of its splendour. Rapt, I dropped my pan and hastened after it. Ahead on the bank I met a Celestial, not panning, but crouching in perfect immobility. Loath to pass him, I stopped and waited for him to move. When he did, it was a most peculiar motion; he cast into the air his own plait. To my further astonishment the plait continued soaring as an angling line uncoiling from a reel. On it stretched, and on, in a wondrous elongation, finally landing with a splash in the river. At the same moment, a monstrous gold tail burst from the water and the Celestial lurched forward violently. Scrambling for purchase among the rocks, he began his tug o' war – a Chinese Jonah against a gilded whale. When I finally awoke, the Celestial reigned triumphant, hauling upon the rocks that priceless catch.

Thus our neighbours' tenacity and good fortune mocked our failure, even in our dreams. We coveted their laughter as they came up from the river, balancing on a pole their teeming baskets. 'Children of the Mother Lode', they had no need for teaspoons; she fed them directly from her paps. Coop called them 'heathen alchemists'. To ascertain their golden secret, he concealed himself near to where they worked, but their method was simple panning, he confoundedly reported, differing from ours in only speed and mirth.

To numb disconsolation and the bombarding effect of Coop's snores, I began to indulge, too, in a nightly tipple. (The sweetness of the whisky I tasted not upon my tongue, but in my thirsting heart. From the first draught I had discovered a thrifty mode of transport; though my love lay a vast distance from me, if I had sufficiently imbibed, when I closed my eyes, I felt her near.) One night as we shuttled the bottle to and fro, an idea, sure as a river stone, struck me on the head. Salvation would come not by angel or Messiah, but in another party of our race. With this end in mind, we agreed that while I panned Coop would keep watch upon the trail. The prospect of delivery cheering us greatly, I allowed myself a double measure of drink.

That night Evaline's tangibility so aroused me, I found myself rolling upon her bosom. Her formidable scent I truly breathed. If these were the delightful workings of an extra dram, I wished I had indulged more frequently! Of a sudden, though, the fancy vanished and I sensed a most unimaginary squeeze. With ardour unmistakable, Coop was gripping me, wheezing hotly on my neck. The last time we had thus entwined had been by the miner's fire a-jigging. The queer semblance (how it had unnerved me then!) now admitted no denial: Coop's embrace and Evaline's were twins. Thus I came to know by experience how loneliness is a dread affliction, worse even than self-disgust.

Gold Mountain, in which I am enlightened to the good
Humanity of our Neighbours

'I AM ILL,' I told Coop. 'I am dying.'
'You don't know their parleyvoo!'
This did not deter me. I set off to the Chinese camp with a need more pressing than even that of gold.

The Celestials had a flock of scabious hens and a garden made from terracing the bank. Approaching, I found a fellow stooping between the rows of greens. 'My bowels have not moved in weeks,' I abashedly confessed. 'Could I beg from you a –?' I gestured to the unfamiliar cousin of our cabbage at his feet.

When he straightened, I saw before me my equal in physical insignificance. He squinted, perplexed, so I pantomimed my complaint. Then he bade me wait as he repaired to their tent. (When he drew aside the flap I saw it stacked inside with blankets.) A moment later he returned with a different cure: a handful of foul-smelling sticks and leaves.

'Tea,' he said in a toothy exhibition.

Within two days this potion had done the trick. In truth, I might have set a watch by my visits to the earth closet. 'Those Celestials are good fellows,' I told Coop.

He spat his whisky on the ground. 'They're little dandies in their pigtails, just like you! That's why you love them!' Then he crawled into the tent and, till morn, blat not a further word.

I was roused as usual by the insistent buzz of flies and the clack of Bruin's jaws as he caught them. Then Coop issued forth his cheery reveille.

'Shite! Shite! Shite!'

He had taken to wearing a lady's bonnet stolen from the dancers. 'It comes to this!' he griped. 'Sluicing dregs with Celestials!'

We were not even sluicing. That required an apparatus we did not possess. I hastened to remind him of this and how we had come unfortunately to land there. Pronouncing me a cretin, he stalked off toward the trail, stopping first to make poor Bruin yelp for mercy.

Since first we fell stranded in the wilderness I had maintained that pleasant manners would keep us civilized and therefore sane. That evening I entered the Celestial camp again. I found them by the fire, watching the progress of a kettle, their voices tolling merrily. Perceiving me, though, they at once ceased conversing. I had come to thank the good apothecary, but unable to tell one from the other, was struck as mum. In the eerie silence, the firelight warped and made sinister their features. Somewhere an owl shrieked. Then one leapt up, jabbed his finger at me and made the cruel pronouncement all men loathe to hear.

'Die... Die.'

I swooned. Luckily one nimble fellow arrested my fall. A second applied himself to my revival by a vigorous fanning of his hat. Then, as a flock of birds will wake in one clamorous burst, they resumed their chatter and in a throng helped me to a seat. Finally I recognized the apothecary as the one whose dire utterance had instilled in me such terror. Now he explained himself, mostly by dumb-show. It was my pallor that had startled them; as I had taken them for my murderers, they had supposed I was a ghost.

Ready in the kettle was a manner of dumpling which they served in bowls with cabbage. Though they kindly pressed this meal upon me, I repeatedly declined, for instead of spoons, they ate with sticks. (These implements, I perceived, required no small dexterity. Had poultry been on the menu, however, or even a fresh egg, I might have happily employed my fingers!) When I accepted tea, served likewise in a bowl, they were satisfied and settled down to eat. I soon surmised that the apothecary alone knew a little English. Lee Hon was his name. The others, though, were eager students. Throughout the meal they used their sticks as pointers, asking how I called things.

'Fire,' I told them. 'Mountain. River. Gold.'

I was not the only tutor. Lee Hon opened wide his arms to embrace the lonely place we inhabited, then taught me its Chinese name. Later I informed Coop, 'We are at Gold Mountain.'

'Ask them then,' he retorted, 'how they are making their mountain of gold!'

I wondered if something in the Chinese camp recalled to me my darling Evaline, or if disillusionment with my own lot endeared them to me. Once I had felt a kinship with Coop, but could no longer abide his crude manners and philosophies. Though we spoke the same language, and glared at one another through same-shaped eyes, I surely did not love him.

In which a good Fellow joins our jolly Company

'WHERE HAVE ALL the men gone?' I asked Coop.

I meant the scores of eager miners rushing off to Cariboo. Coop's post on the trail served the hope that we might accost a passing party, yet not a soul had he encountered, not even Natives who I had understood were numerous in these parts. This had begun to irk me as much as the flies and the stones that made their unaccountable entry into my boots. One unprofitable afternoon I therefore put away my pan and clambered up the slope to spy on Coop. I found him nowhere on the trail, but in the wood slumbering behind a tree. Shaking him to consciousness by his slobbery bonnet strings, I roared an ultimatum. Until he came with news of fellow panners, he was banished from the camp; I would henceforth bring his supper to the trail. When he failed to appear that night, I was truly astonished, marvelling that he had actually paid me heed. Then I settled happily into a solitude infinitely less lonely than keeping vexatious company.

Two nights hence I woke to Bruin baying in mortal terror and a frightful crashing in the trees. Both I and the Celestial party dashed from our tents with lanterns lit hastily. Upright and staggering toward us was a maddened and vociferous bear. I held the musket but, ignorant of its workings, stood with clacking knees. With great relief I espied a familiar gleam: the bear was wearing shoes.

He was drunk beyond language (which accounted for his animal roars) and miserably tattered. Coop by then had caught up and together we cajoled him to our tent.

'There he is,' said Coop when we had tucked him in. 'Yer good fellow.'

The following day, when our visitor had regained his wits, Coop recounted to him his words. 'Samuel Goodfellow,' the stranger rejoined, his grin so blackened he might lately have supped on charcoal. 'That's sure enough my name.'

I did not believe him. To pry from him a little of his history, I enquired after his excellent and grossly incongruous shoes.

'I kilt a man for 'em in Californee, but it was hardly worth it. They pinch me in the heels.'

Describing the rising Hostilities in and among the Camps.
Revealing also a Scheme of mine and how It is thrown over
for One better. Further, the Account of the Death of a certain
Character for which the Reader will require a Handkerchief

THE PRESENCE OF the Celestial fowl grieved us all, having known for too long only salt pork for meat. Bruin especially coveted them. (Once daring to enter the Celestial camp, he had been soundly thrashed by Coop.) When Goodfellow joined our company, Bruin's ration became his and Bruin was forced to seek sustenance for himself. Mainly he gnawed our boots, his bulk daily diminishing until love of life surpassed his love of Coop and he went and got himself a hen. Goodfellow, witness to the deed, pursued Bruin and wrested away his banquet. After the manner of the best French chefs, he and Coop impaled it on a stick and roasted it in its feathery jacket. For

Bruin's trouble, they tossed him the well-sucked bones.

That night one of the Chinese burst into our camp accompanied by all his fury. Brandishing a knife and with choppy gesticulation, he informed us he was full prepared to quarter Bruin. Goodfellow, by way of rebuttal, issued forth a sonorous belch.

Soon afterward, I found a sign fixed to a tree outside our camp.

Nottiss! To Seleteels!
You are Hearbi noteefed that iff
yo gow intu this camp
you will ketch hell!

That my own name was not recorded there surprised me. Despite a certain handshake, Coop and Goodfellow were now rightful partners – in sloth instead of gold – and I, I was their object of derision. They retorted upon me noisome slander: if I polished my boots or performed ablutions in the river, I was a 'dandy' or a 'maid'. For my acquaintance with Lee Hon, they called me 'Hen Ree'.

I loved that sobriquet. My few visits to the Chinese camp had been my only peace. Once, wretched with a longing for Evaline, I had crossed over and like the peddler that I had been, put on display the woeful contents of my heart. I had not expected comprehension, just a sympathetic ear, yet Lee Hon rose and went into the tent. He fetched a tin box and from it took a daguerreotype of his wife. Her hair was pulled tight in the Celestial plait and she wore a striking costume: flowered slippers fitting to tread the ground of the Flowery Kingdom (Lee Hon's name for China), a short jacket that fastened at the side, and, I am decidedly not mistaken – trousers.

Since Goodfellow's arrival and the incident with the hen, my relations with the Celestials had ailed. Lee Hon no longer saluted me if we happened to meet at the river and I dared not pay a visit to their camp. Something cheered me though. With Evaline's map as my true guide I intended to try again for Cariboo. My breast pocket a bank, I had a modest account, enough to quit Gold Mountain. The gold was rightly mine – flake by flake I had extracted it – though Coop and Goodfellow were sure to call it common wealth. My departure would therefore be stealthy; I had already begun to squirrel provisions in the woods.

From my bed by the fire (having been thus displaced), I watched a shadow-show on the tent wall: Coop and Goodfellow, card-sharpers, cheating one another. With no gold to wager, they played for punitive stakes – the winner bashing the loser on the pate. One evening, in the course of this jollification, Coop and Goodfellow began a suspiciously subdued colloquy.

'We'll kill the lot of 'em,' was what reached my ears. I sat up alarmed. From the Celestial camp, I could see a fire still burning.

It being so far into night, I had expected to find them reposing, but they were busily at work. Onto several blankets, spread out on the ground, they were pouring silt from sacks.

'They plan to take your hens!' I cried, translating with gesticulation.

They stopped short and gaped at me. Then Lee Hon came forward with an exaggerated grin and took me by the arm. 'Thank you, Hen Ree,' he told me and began to steer me off. Glancing over my shoulder, I saw the others hastening to conceal their occupation. I realized then that Coop had been correct; steady toil alone did not enrich them. I had chanced upon their secret art.

I clutched Lee Hon's hand. 'Show me. I beg you, show me.'

Why he conceded, I do not know. Perhaps it was to return the favour I had done them in my warning, or that I had already seen the greater part of it. It occurred to me also that there might be a fondness between us, despite his being a Celestial and I a Ghost.

The more they stoked the fire, the hungrier it grew, many-tongued, lapping at the night. A glittering silt, a fortnight's panning, they spread across the blankets. When folded, these blankets and their contents became their noble offering and by way of rite were fed into the flames. I was awe-struck. In this simple method I fancied a golden enchantment, heard in their unfathomable parlance incantation. Now I know no manner of utterance can speed or slow this truth: anything fire loves will burn. For fire has a mouth and a thousand teeth and its bite is all-transforming. In the slow-burning the tiny flakes amalgamated to nuggets. At dawn we sifted through the cool ash, retrieving in handfuls the metamorphosed gold.

My second plan for Cariboo I then abandoned and applied myself to panning with reborn hope. Compared to my previous exacting labour – gleaning pure flake – collecting the silt required little wit. In truth, as I panned a pleasant drowsiness ofttimes suffused me, almost as if I dreamt awake. Then, gazing at the swirling contents of my pan, I would behold an image. Formed not of gold or gravel, they were visions, as in the tales of prophets and saints. I saw, for example, my mother back in England mixing soda tonic for her wind. Also revealed: the ideal shoe. Evaline I saw dreaming, and then I saw her dream. In my half-dream she was smiling at her own dream – at ladies dressed in breeches and fellows wearing plaits.

One morning a raucous commotion from the Celestial camp broke off my reverie. Leaving my pan, I raced to learn the trouble, stood watching from a safe vantage behind a tree. The Celestials were shouting and waving cudgel-like their fists. Lee Hon, in the centre of the camp, was clutching fast to Bruin's tail while Bruin, fuelled by famine and oblivious to his passenger, was pursuing in crazed circles a shrieking hen. This carousel of starvation continued its merry rotations until the fowl finally collapsed. Immediately, Bruin seized hold of his feast. But a second Celestial pounced likewise upon Bruin and with no ado whatsoever plunged into his wasted scruff a knife.

Coop and Goodfellow, also witnesses to this carnage, were strangely gleeful. Coop refused to bury Bruin. He left the corpse to rot under his warning sign, saying the Gold Commissioner would soon pass by and bring justice to the river. Hitherto I would not have believed the flies could plague us worse. Blue-bottles swirled over the swelling carcass, an opaque confusion. In the autumn heat, Bruin's bursting open was the crack of doom.

An Account of the scandalous Trial and its Fatal Repercussions.
Also, my Experience with the Celestial Method of Gold
Retrieval and What was caught in Justice's Pan

'THIS WAS DAMSHUR more an angel than a dog!' Coop told the Gold Commissioner who had appeared while on his route downstream. 'In cold blood they kilt 'im!' By then Bruin's bones were protruding whitely from his putrid flesh. Bending over to examine them, the Commissioner gagged behind his handkerchief.

'And Yer Highness, look what they done to Coop!' Goodfellow cried. Coop drew from his pocket a bandaged hand; Goodfellow proceeded to unswaddle it. Then Coop, bawling, a debauched baby in his bonnet, thrust in the Commissioner's face his freshly scored and bleeding stumps.

The Gold Commissioner is the lawful adjudicator of all disputes under fifty English pounds. He seemed a just enough fellow, albeit haggard and with one eye listing sightless in its socket. Declaring Bruin worth two pounds and Coop's severed fingers ten pounds apiece, he drew his pistol and rounded up the terrified Celestials. Having assembled on the river bank both disputing parties, he produced a Bible and set to swearing in the Christians. Coop repeated his libellous testimony with Goodfellow's perfidious corroboration, but since the Celestials could neither utter a language intelligible to the Commissioner, nor be sworn to oath, their defence was disqualified.

I then proceeded to describe in exacting detail how Bruin came to lose his life, for just reason and with due warning. The Commissioner turned his blind eye to me.

'Surely, sir,' I protested, 'you won't take the word of these vulgarians over that of honest gentlemen!'

'Having no words from them, how can I presume honesty? Furthermore, your title 'gentlemen' is the grossest of misnomers. Do you know who these pathetic fellows are?'

I looked to the Celestials, tattered and made even more diminutive by incomprehension and fear. It occurred to me then that I more truly belonged in their party than my own. In truth, welling up inside me was a new allegiance which I now felt called upon to defend. I turned to the Commissioner.

'They are my friends, sir.'

'They are slaves,' he retorted, 'indentured to a coolie broker to repay their passage to this hell! Imagine the hell they come from, if they would go to such expense! And now I shall fine them, Mr Merritt, for their injury to this man, thus happily prolonging their misery!' He broke off coughing.

'They are innocent of your charge, sir, and my testimony will prove it!' I paused to let him finish retching. His handkerchief, I noted, was stained with bloody sputum. 'I had several occasions to remark Mr Coop's stumps before we ever came in contact with Celestials.'

'When, Mr Merritt?'

'We shook to seal our bargain before we set out for Cariboo. Once, too, I comforted him as he wept.'

'Lies!' screamed Coop.

'We danced together! He was a lady and I a fellow!'

Now Goodfellow, too, set to railing, but the Commissioner objected. 'Mr Coop and Mr Goodfellow! I shall question this witness without interruption or molestation! Do you mark my words?'

Coop shrunk down in obeisance; Goodfellow expectorated on the ground.

'At any other time,' the Commissioner continued, 'did you note Mr Coop's disfigurement?'

This question caused me to blush deeply, but having laid my hand upon the Bible, I was fettered to the truth. The matter of Coop's and my nocturnal tussling, of which we ourselves had never spoken, I now shame-facedly confessed.

'You say he squeezed you?' queried the flabbergasted Commissioner.

'Aye, sir, he did.'

'How often?'

'While we shared a tent, sir, almost every night.'

(Here Coop and Goodfellow, with violent expletives, renewed their denials, but were silenced once again by threat of contempt of court.)

'And, Mr Merritt, did you enjoy this treatment?' asked the Commissioner.

'It gave a bit of comfort, sir. I miss so much my lady.'

'A moment ago you called Mr Coop a lady.' Then the Commissioner, disgust marring his countenance, dismissed my evidence on the grounds that I was unsound of mind. His judgement: the Celestials were without a doubt guilty of the aforementioned crimes. The confiscation of their gold and its disbursement among the Commissioner and the aggrieved plaintiffs was the swiftest retribution.

Coop and Goodfellow were equally swift in leading the Commissioner to the Celestials' tent and their unsecret cache. Then erupted a most hellish skirmish as the Chinese tried to defend their store. Clearly Lee Hon did not understand my part in these outrageous proceedings; when I approached him, he drew a knife.

I fast retreated to the safety of the nearby trees, but my nostrils were immediately assailed by a potent stench – Bruin's corrupting carcass billowing gas. Although all the men found sufficient air with which to fuel their fight, it nearly stifled me. I fled the tainted atmosphere, stumbling up the wooded slope.

Waiting on the trail was the Commissioner's horse. I grabbed its halter and was about to take up the unlikely trade of pony stealing, when I heard shots fired at the river. I could not go without learning my friends' fate, though nearly an hour passed before the Commissioner reached the trail.

'Who is shot?' I asked.

'Celestials. The whole party.'

'Take me with you!' I implored him, feeling my breast pocket for a bribe. To my immense shock I found it empty, all my earnings scattered on the slope. 'Sir, I beg you! Take me!'

'Where I am going, Mr Merritt,' the Commissioner replied, 'I will no other man to go.'

I watched him ride away. I could not run myself, for night was settling like a million flies. Nor did the prospect of the morning's light offer any hope; I was penniless and without a morsel. Coop and Goodfellow, in possession at last of real stakes, would shuffle and deal through the night. Already I could hear their roisterous carousing far below. I felt certain they would not welcome a third player.

In the end I huddled upon the trail, insensible with shock and grief. Above me the constellations were like minuscule flecks of gold set in everlasting patterns in the firmament. As I crouched, I fell to wondering why the Chinese were called Celestials, whether it was their shaved forelocks that earned them the appellation – their naked brows round and smooth like planets – or that, when smiling, their eyes folded into pleasing crescents that brought to mind the waning moon. They had, too, tails like black comets and voices that mimicked the tonal music of the spheres. Then the stars themselves, indeed the whole bespangled sky, seemed to unswirl in an astronomical tribute to my friends. Lying back to watch this wonder, I drifted off to sleep.

In my dream, Smoke Personified was leaning over me in an oppressive cloak of black, forcing up my nose its ghastly fingers. I woke gasping. Below in the darkness, gold sparks were shooting. I saw them glinting, as in my pan, but would not touch them, lest I burn: *something in our camp had caught on fire.* The tent. Blazing up of a sudden, it made a mighty pyre, Coop and Goodfellow trapped within.

If the compound of feelings churning in me could have been distilled, it would have made an insanity potion. At once I battered my skull against a tree and hummed a ditty I had learned upon the trail. ('We are dancing girls in Cariboo, and we're liked by all the men...') Then, thinking of Coop's corpse braising in the embers, I set to wailing, only to find myself a moment later jigging. Thus I passed the remainder of that hellish night.

At daybreak, exhausted and in awful trepidation, I ventured back down the slope. About their camp the Chinese lay in various wracked postures, all bearing monstrous wounds. Lee Hon's very arm was severed from his person as he stared heavenward from a pool of gore. I turned away in horror. They were the sole men with whom I had felt affinity, perhaps in all my sorry life. Now they had travelled on to a place not even Evaline could map.

As for Coop and Goodfellow – drunk, they must have knocked the lamp down in the tent while gambling their booty. I knelt beside the fire's remains. The Celestials' gold, twice-consumed by flame, had fused to weighty nuggets. I might have been a rich man. I might have made my love a ring. But gold washed in blood loses all its lustre, makes an ugly trinket and a foul currency. To fund my escape, I was obliged to take a handful. A more grisly chore I cannot imagine, combing through those ashes, sorting gold from charred stubs of bone.

Wherein I arrive back in Everlasting,
greatly down at the Heel

BY THE TIME I found my Evaline snow lay upon the ground and I was a tatterdemalion, as much a pauper as when I left her. In my absence she seemed to have accumulated flesh, that or trial and hunger had shrivelled me. And though she greeted me with the same bashful manner I adored, I saw at once I had not been missed. Knowing well she would refuse me, nonetheless I begged her hand, then with my tears I washed her boots.

'It would be too comic, Mr Merritt,' she told me. 'As if I were the man and you the lady.'

At least she consented to make for me a map. She shooed me to her bed and while I tumbled headlong in its frowzy comfort, she made a coy show of removing her hair pins and letting her plait fall down her back.

'What if I can no longer dream?' I asked her.

'How do you know you are not dreaming now?' Turning, she smiled at me in the lamp-light and for a moment I thought she was Coop.

How true her words! What had happened to me awake was infinitely more terrible and strange than anything I had encountered in a nightmare. As a lad I was wont to contemplate the simple workings of a boot-lace, how eye-to-eye it made its criss-cross pattern – certain, predetermined and everlasting. So too, I had thought, would be my life. Now even elemental truths – justice, for example, or what defines a race of people, or even, for that matter, a man or woman – all this seemed to me reversed. I was lost and knew not where to go. We slept like babes and, in dreaming, awoke together to find ourselves upon a forest trail. This sylvan path we trod but a short distance before it opened in a field. In truth, we had reached a vista glittering and vast – a plain of golden stars. Evaline turned to me in amazement. 'This is the Celestial Route!' And so I learned my proper destination. I took her hand, she took mine, and as one we ventured forth. In the morn she sat up in the bed, her visage radiant with our shared dream. 'Such a lovely place!' she exclaimed. 'Are you certain it exists?'

Now I am waiting out the winter in a room above the saloon, replying to my mother's bombastic correspondence, taking her pennies to pay my keep. Sometimes I wax despondent, lamenting what has happened to me and my boots. Mostly, though, I pass the hours studying Evaline's map of China, its mighty wall, the two great rivers wending to the sea. Somehow it stirs me. It seems as much a work of art as of cartography. When first I saw it, I proposed she travel with me to be sure that this time I would not stray off course. She only laughed and told me she could sojourn far more economically.

My boots! Of the original laces, only one remains; the left I now fasten with a bit of string. Part of the stacking on that heel is also gone, giving me a most ungainly limp. As for the right, being so punctured by Bruin's gnawing it would make a perfect sieve. Yet these mean scraps of leather have brought me so great a distance I am loath now to part with them. If they endure this one last journey, then I shall retire them – for a pair of flowered slippers.

THE CHMARNYK

IN 1906, after scorching the Dakota sky, an asteroid fell to earth and struck and killed a dog. Only a mutt, but Baba said, 'Omen.' It was her dog. They crossed the border into safety, into Canada. But the next spring was strange in Manitoba, alternating spells of heat and cold. One bright day Mama went to town, stood before a shop window admiring yard goods, swaddled infant in her arms. From the eaves above a long glimmering icicle gave up its hold, dropped like a shining spear. The baby was impaled.

These misfortunes occurred before I was born. I learned them from tongues, in awe, as warnings. My brother Teo said, 'Every great change is wrought in the sky.'

Grieving, they fled Manitoba, just another cursed place. Open wagon, mattresses baled, copper pots clanking. Around the neck of the wall-eyed horse two things: cardboard picture of the Sacred Heart; cotton strip torn from Baba's knickers. Every morning as she knotted the cloth, she whispered in the twitching ear, 'As drawers cover buttocks, cover those evil eyes!' Thus protected, that old horse carried them right across Saskatchewan. In Alberta it fell down dead.

So they had to put voice to what they had feared all along: the land wasn't cursed, they were. More exactly, Papa. A reasonable man most of the time, he had these spells, these ups and downs. Up, he could throw off his clothes and tread a circular path around the house knee-deep through snow. Or he would claim to be speaking English when, in fact, he was speaking in tongues. 'English, the language of Angels!' but no one understood him. Down, he lay on the hearth, deathly mute, Baba spoon-feeding him, Teo and Mama saying the rosary. I was just a baby when he died.

But this is a story about Teo, dead so many years. I remember him stocky and energetic, his streaky blond hair. If they had stayed in Galicia, he would have been a *chmarnyk*, a rain-man. In the Bible, Pharaoh had a dream that seven gaunt cows came out of the river to feed on cattails. He dreamed of seven ears of corn on a single stalk, withered and blighted by east wind. But Teo never relied on the auguries of sleep. He could read the sky.

'Rain on Easter Day and the whole summer is wet. If you see stars in the morning from one to three, the price of wheat rises.'

He told me this in a field still bound by old snow. He had stood out there the whole night and I was calling him to Easter Mass, 1929. 'What'll it be this year then, smartie?'

'Drought.' He pronounced the word like he was already thirsty. 'Little sister, listen. The sky is only as high as the horizon is far.'

'Well, la-di-da.'

Teo was nineteen, I twelve, and the skin of my own dry lips cracked as I echoed: 'drought'. All that spring, smoke rose straight out of chimneys and every evening the sky flared. 'That's dust in the air already. That's dry weather,' he said.

Always reading, he got an idea about the cattail. 'Ten times more edible tubers per acre than a crop of potatoes.'

'Just before a storm,' he said, 'you can see the farthest.'

Since the price of wheat was not going to rise, Teo sold our farm and bought the store in town. There I learned our other names: 'bohunk' and 'garlic-eater'. People didn't like owing us money, but the fact that they did never stopped them writing in the newspaper that we couldn't be loyal subjects of the British Empire. That we would never learn to put saucers under our cups. I refused to wear my embroidered blouses and sometimes even turned to the wall the cardboard picture of the Sacred Heart. It embarrassed me the way Our Saviour bared his sweet breast, as if he didn't care what people thought of him.

Teo was unperturbed. There was work to be done and I could be his little helper. At Mud Lake, by then half receded, ringed by white alkali scum, he asked me to remove my clothes. Covering my breasts with spread-open hands, I waded in, then clung to a snag slippery with algae while Teo, on shore, named clouds.

'Cumulus. Cumulus. Cumulus.'

'Why me?' I shouted.

'Needs a virgin,' he called. 'A smooth thigh.'

I came out festooned with leeches – arms, legs, shoulder even. He chose the halest one and burned the rest off with his cigarette. All the way home I wore that guzzling leech sheltered in a wet handkerchief. Like a doting mother I nursed it. Then we put it in a Mason jar with water and a little stick.

'Leech barometer,' Teo said. 'Fair weather when the leech stays in the water. Unless the leech is dead.'

The next year Mud Lake had disappeared. Rising out of what once was water – a secret charnel-house. Old glowing buffalo bones.

Already farms were being seized. Some families had been paying us in chits since 1929. To one farmer Teo made a gift – an idea expressed to hide the giving. 'If he wanted, a man might collect and sell those bones as fertilizer.' We saw the farmer working every day. On first sight of the bones his horse had spooked. Now it had to be blindfolded – led like a reluctant bride through the sweltering town, an antimacassar the veil on its head. It strained with the cart, load white and rattling. Vertebrae fell in puffs of dust on the road, provoking feud amongst the forsaken dogs.

I never knew there could be so much death in one place or that the labour of removing it could be so gruelling. Finally, all the bones in a dry heap at the train station, ready to be loaded. Women could go down and have their photograph taken with a huge skull in their lap. Boys swung at each other with the leg bones.

Strangest railway robbery anybody had ever heard of. Overnight it all vanished. Not even a tooth left on the platform. The exhausted farmer lost his remuneration. After that he posted himself in front of the store warning those who entered that Teo was not as stupid as he looked. Declaring revenge was a man's right when he thirsted for justice. He spat so often on our window I made a routine of cleaning it off. The pattern of saliva on the dusty glass was like cloudburst.

It was so dry in the Palliser Triangle dunes of dust stopped the trains. We tucked rags around doors and window sills, blew black when we blew into our handkerchiefs. In Galicia, Teo would have been a *chmarnyk*, a rain-man. He took me with him, driving where roads were passable, farm to farm. Waiting in the car, I watched him point at the sky. Children circled, staring in at me. They thumbed their noses and wrote 'garlic' in the dust on the windscreen. I kept my gaze on Teo as he exhorted skeletal-faced farmers to send their wives and daughters into the fields. Send them into the fields on Sunday morning and have them urinate, for a woman's urine has power to cause rain.

Brandishing brooms, they drove him off their porches. They kicked him in the seat of the pants.

'Why are we doing this?' I cried. His every good deed bred animosity.

Teo said, 'They didn't know Our Saviour either.' To give me faith, he made a drop of water appear at the end of his nose, glistening like a glass rosary bead. 'That's without even trying,' he said.

Nobody went into the fields, of course. Just Mama and Baba. And me, squatting, skirts hoisted. I saw my urine pool in the dust, ground too parched to drink. High in a tree a crow was watching me. It shouted down that rain comes at a cost, and even then might not come for good.

In the Bible, Pharaoh dreamed of seven gaunt cows. By 1932, I must have seen seven hundred so much worse than gaunt. Angular with starvation or dead and bloated, legs straight up in the air.

'Ten times more edible tubers per acre in a crop of cattails than a crop of potatoes!'

'Who told you that?'

'And the fluff! That's good insulation! Mattress stuffing,

quilt batting! From the stalks, wallboard and paper! The leaves
– baskets, clothing!'

I laughed. Who would wear a cattail? 'How come nobody
ever thought of this before, smartie?'

'Lots nobody ever thought of! Every great change is
wrought in the sky! God made the cattail!' His tongue raced,
arms circled in the air.

But the big idea was cheap cattle feed, deliverance from
famine. Teo the Deliverer. 'Is a cow going to eat a cattail root?'
I wanted to know.

'Cows eating pieces off tractors! Cows eating gate latches!'
Hardware disease.

And the next morning he drove away from the Palliser Triangle, northward, looking for a cattail slough. I waited. Baba
sucked on her bare gums all day, as if that way she could wet
her throat. Mama – always the same stories. 'Dakota. 1906. A
good doggie.' She raised one fist in the air, swept it down with
a loud smack into her outstretched palm. Weeping, she mimed
the baby in her arms. That lance of ice, it dropped right out of
heaven.

Then this, another sorrow: how Papa died. As a child I
thought he'd been plucked from the plough and raptured
straight on high. Mama used to tell how she had clutched his
ankle and dangled in mid-air trying hold him back. Nothing
could be further from the truth. He threw himself on a pitch-
fork. So much blood, it was like when they killed a pig. This
she confessed in the back room of the store as I sat on a lard
pail. Suicide triples a curse.

On a red background I appliquéd a cattail. The words: THE
EVERYTHING PLANT. For batting I planned to use the brown
and gold pollen of the cattail flower. We were going to string it
across the back of the car when we, brother and sister, did our
tour of the drought towns, made our presentation at the feed
stores. We were going to sleep under it at night. I was Teo's
little helper.

In the corner of every eye, a plug of dust. I was afraid of crying, of someone licking the water off my face.

I urinated again in a field.

There were no clouds to name.

Now they said we were worse than Jews, almost as bad as Chinamen. I had never seen either. On the counter they scattered handfuls of raisins, railing, 'Stones! Stones!' as if they actually paid us. What could we do about fly-infested flour, rancid bacon, the desiccated mouse in the sugar? When the cash register opened, chits flew out like a hundred moths. On all these accusing faces the dirty lines were a map of the roads Teo had gone away on.

Now we wanted Teo to take us away. Baba said she could smell hatred. It smelled like gunpowder.

In Galicia, Mama said, Drought is a beautiful woman. She persuades a young peasant to carry her on his back. Wherever he goes crops wither and die, ponds evaporate, birds, songs stuck in their throats, drop out of trees. Horrified, he struggles to loosen the cinch of her legs round his waist, her grappling hands at his neck. In the end, to be rid of his burden, he leaps from a bridge. Drought dries up the river instantly and, crashing on the rocks below, our young peasant breaks opens his head.

Finally a package. Inside, a big tuberous finger, hairy and gnarled. We marvelled it was still wet.

'What is it?' Mama asked.

'A cattail root.'

When Baba touched it, she started to cry. What did it mean? Would Teo come for us? Alive, it was holding the rain. That night, to keep it moist, I brought it to bed and put it inside me.

To cure fever, drink whisky with ground garlic. Eat bread wrapped in cobwebs. But I did not think it was fever. Overnight my hair had curled like vetch tendrils and my head throbbed where a horse had kicked me seven years before. Beside my bed, the leech barometer. So many years in the jar, I had thought the leech was dead. Now it shimmied out of the water and halfway up the stick.

Mama said, looking over the town, 'Smoke from all these

chimneys curling down.' When I would not take the bread and whisky, she pulled my hair.

Just before a storm, you can see the farthest. We saw you coming miles away. Dust-maker, you were weaving all over the road, horn pressed. By the time we got Baba down the stairs and into the street, a crowd had gathered round the car. You were standing on the hood, almost naked, wet skirt of cat-tail leaves pasted to your thighs.

Mama gasped, 'Teo has his father's curse.'

The sere voice of a crow: *rain costs.*

And I was part to blame. I had given my innocence to a cat-tail root while you held its power.

From the beating part of your chest, your brow, water had begun to trickle, ribboning downward, the sheen of moisture all across you. Motionless, arms open, fingers spread and dripping – you were sowing rain. We were sweating too, the day dry and searing, but soon you were dissolving, hair saturated, nostrils and eyes streaming culverts. Then you turned, spun round and spattered the silent crowd. Turned again, kept spinning, faster. Whirling, whirling on the slippery hood, you drenched and astounded us, became a living fountain. And then, amazing! A nimbus, seven-coloured, shimmering all around you.

In Galicia, when thunder sounds, prostrate yourself to save your soul. That day thunder discharged, a firearm, reverberating. Mama and Baba dropped to the ground. A dark curtain was drawn across the Palliser Triangle. Black geyser sky.

You bowed forward and vomited a river.

The crowd fell back. They had never seen a *chmarnyk*.

After Teo made it rain, the whole town was filled with steam, water evaporating off the streets and the wet backs of the men who carried Teo's body away. Dogs staggered out of cover to drink from temporary puddles. And in all the fields, green shoots reared, only to wither later in the reborn drought.

They carried Teo's body away and wouldn't let us see him. 'Struck by lightning,' they said. How could we argue? I was only fifteen and neither Mama nor Baba could speak English.

The moment he was taken, we had been rolling on the ground. But I remember clearly the presence of that farmer, the one robbed of his charnel-house, his smile like lightning. The English word 'shotgun' never had a place on my tongue.

Years later Teo came to Mama in a dream. In the dream he had a hole in his chest big enough to climb into, gory as the Sacred Heart. 'I have seen the face of Our Saviour,' he told her. 'He lets me spit off the clouds.'

As for me, two things at least I know. The cattail root holds more than water. Every great change is wrought in the sky.

BREAD AND STONE

IF NAN TOOK another man he could not be like her husband Patrick. She did not want to delude herself into loving for mere resemblance. Also she had Lucifer Bill to consider. He claimed to remember his father, though she, sceptic, thought it was from the photographs, the stories she told. She was glad, though, that he hadn't turned out to despise Patrick for his absence, his untimely blameless death. Honour thy father and thy mother. That is what they had been doing the past four years. She had lost her own mother in the same accident and Joni, her only daughter.

The first time she went out with Stephen, she knew he was enough unlike Patrick. But she had met a lot of people who were repelled by tragedy and wasn't sure if Stephen would be, too. So she told it all. 'We usually spent Christmas with Patrick's people. That year, though, Bill had to have a few tests at the hospital. Nothing serious, he was just, even at age two, how can I put it?' She made a gesture with her hands – pure energy.

'Frisky?'

'You're kind. Manic I was going to say. Anyway, Patrick and Joni and my mother drove up together. Bill and I stayed back, so we weren't in the car when it happened. End of story.'

He didn't press her, but when he took her home, asked to see Bill. Nan agreed enthusiastically; meeting an unconscious Bill was his best introduction. They crept up the stairs. As soon as she opened the door and looked at the room through someone else's eyes, she regretted it. Chaos and upheaval. Her son was a vandal.

He was in a pyjama top, crosswise on the bed, bare bottom glowing in the yellow light of his night lamp. A heat-maker, he warmed himself by his own inner fire and even in winter could not tolerate too much blanket.

'Cute little fellow.'

'Little? He's a monster for his age.'

'Where'd he get the red?'

'His father's beard. Joni was even brighter.'

Downstairs a wedding picture hung in the hallway. 'Your husband was a bear,' he said.

And this man Stephen, Nan decided, was a stag. Fine and sleek. She liked the way he kissed her cheek, not her lips, and even then on the porch. Not in front of a photograph of Patrick.

Then she worried that since she had told Stephen the severed story of her life he would be too familiar; even now she didn't want to hear Joni's name spoken as someone might name an object or a person gone out of the room. Or, worse, he might feign an ingratiating comprehension. So when they next met for a walk in the ravine, to prevent his disappointing her, she brought the subject up again.

'I told him they all joined hands and went to heaven.'

'And he believed?'

'Of course. But he resents not having visiting rights.'

When he asked what she believed in, she answered: doubt. 'But I was raised Quaker. Silently.' Little maxims always rang in her ear. Joy cometh in the morning. Where your treasure is, there will your heart be. What man, if his son asks bread, will give him a stone?

After a colourless winter, each unfolding leaf seemed intensely green. The ravine was ringing with the sound of running water. Below, chunks of old snow slid down the thawing bank into the river.

Dinner at Stephen's. She showed Bill how to carry the cake box by the string so the icing would not touch the cardboard. Stephen answered the door, squeezed her hand, squatted to Bill's level.

'How do you do?'

'Monkey poo,' said Bill, deadpan.

'That's a game we play.' She was exhausted from being sly all day long with Bill. Napping and fawning had put him in his behavioral prime, but he was already wandering toward the living room, the tranced steps of a child bent on exploration. A minute in the kitchen doorway with an eye on each man, then she slipped over to the stove.

'Smells wonderful.'

Stephen put in her hands a glass of wine, lifted his own glass, dipped a finger. 'Something special for Bill.'

'What?'

'None of your business.'

She laughed and at the same moment that she kissed him, his finger set the rim of the wine glass singing.

'Nan!' Bill cried from the doorway. 'What are you doing?'

'Stephen's playing music on his glass, that's all.'

They sat down to dinner. Bill gazed at her wistfully, pulling on his lip. Her playful, under-the-table kick offended him. Stephen brought a little pizza.

'Look, Bill,' said Nan. 'Red tomato cheeks. His nose is made of broccoli. Thank you, Stephen.'

'I admit I'm trying to impress you, Bill.'

'*I'm* impressed,' she said.

They ate well, finished a bottle of wine. Bill even used his napkin. While Stephen made coffee she asked Bill to bring the cake to the table. He sat on her lap, solemnly untying and opening the box. 'William Lucifer,' she whispered, kissing his red head, thinking: this is my beloved son in whom I am well pleased. She was not used to wine.

'The cake is just for you and me, right, Nanny?'

'It's for Stephen, too.'

'Stephen didn't share with me.'

'He made you something special. You wouldn't have liked the spicy food we ate.'

'Nanny?' Earnest, innocent voice. 'Stephen stinks, doesn't he?'

She put her hand over her face and thought, Oh God, but when she looked up, Stephen was laughing.

'Bouncing around in the back seat like Wolf-Boy being driven to the vet. Sit down, Romulus, I cry.' Stephen re-enacting the scene in her living room.

'Oh, God. I'm sorry.'

'We get there, Bill slavering – '

She had to laugh.

'Popcorn! Popcorn! I buy him a monster bag. We take our seats. The movie hasn't been rolling five minutes when I look at your boy beside me and see he's stuffing it up his nose!'

'Oh, God!'

'Bill, I say. I only want to direct him to the correct orifice, but he accidentally inhales. Cawing! Caterwauling! We spend half the film in the john blowing blood and snot and popcorn out of his nose.'

'Why don't you sit down? I'll rub your back.'

'Back in our seats, I'm concentrating on the film, trying to fill the thirty-minute gap in the plot. Suddenly I realize – '

She gasped. 'He wasn't there!'

'Slippery little beggar. Gave me the old chase routine. To get him back to the car I had to sling him screaming blue over my shoulder, everybody staring like I'm some child abuser.'

'Last week he bit a girl at kindergarten.'

Stephen slumped on the couch, groaning. 'Is something wrong with Bill? It would help if I knew. A changeling maybe? The Future Ruler of the World?'

'Bill was wild even in the womb. When I was pregnant with him, I turned from vegetarian to raging carnivore. Then, after he was born...' She could laugh about it now. 'We took him to psychiatrists and allergists, exorcists. The conclusion is character. He'll grow out of it. Patrick's mother isn't fazed. She says Patrick was worse.'

'I don't know how you do it.'

'He's tamed me.'

'I'm still game on a package deal, Nan. The two of you, I mean. Even after today – would you believe it?'

That night was the first she let someone lie where Patrick had slept. She didn't feel she had dishonoured him in her mind or body and there was no confusion over whom she touched and moved with or why. But she told Stephen she didn't want him there in the morning. He slipped away, honourable lover, saying he understood.

Bill telling her, 'Patrick could do everything. He built houses and played guitar and made bowls.'

'Wooden bowls on the lathe. You've seen Patrick's guitar, but you don't remember his playing.'

'Nanny, I do! *Dear Abby dear Abby I never thought me and my girlfriend'd ever get caught.* He could get a fish with an arrow!'

'Mexico. Patrick speared fish in the Sea of Cortez. You were hardly two.'

She wondered how far back she could go. Certainly not to her own father, dead of cancer before she could know him. Her mother had always been her friend, even in adolescence. No dog-fights or power struggles. Other kids said: Nan's mum's not from this planet. How far back? She closed her eyes that night and tried, unwound her memory until it stopped at Nan on the sidewalk, aged four, finally able to skip rope, but backwards. Her mother, far away on the steps, is clapping. Stopped next at Nan in her bed. On the ceiling pieces of glinting tin-foil map the constellations. She grips her mother's soft arms, agony, curiosity – please, mummy, please, how was I born? But the room is too dark to see her face. No memorial then for a woman who salved so well the sting of growing.

She never asked why her mother didn't marry again. Now needed the secret reasoning. Not that her mother would have given it if she were alive. The first time Nan made a pie on her own she used a cup of salt. I shouldn't rush, she said, spitting up on her plate. I should be more careful. Her mother said, not have-you-learned-your-lesson-then, but, I rush too much myself. Later Nan remembered that her mother had watched her working and must have seen the motions of her mistake. Seen, but knew: patience leads to experience, and experience, hope.

The yard was lit by stars and the red spiral glow of mosquito coils. They were waiting for the aurora borealis.

'How long is Patrick going to mind? What's the difference – my going to bed with you, my staying the night?'

'Not Patrick. Bill sometimes comes in during the night. He collects me in the morning... There!'

It had begun, the vault and shiver, luminous unpleating of the night sky. Without speaking, they watched. Then she confessed, 'I cleared you out a drawer ages ago.'

The next morning she woke to Lucifer Bill standing at the side of the bed, naked, knocking on her shoulder. He was tiptoe, craning over her, staring at the occupied space. 'Who's that?'

'Who do you think it is?'

'It's not Stephen!' He made a face.

'Do you want to come in?'

'Yuk!' He shook loose his wrist and ran out of the room. A moment later, a symphonic crash of pots and pans. She got up, put on her housecoat and went downstairs to the kitchen.

'What are you doing, jaybird?'

He wouldn't answer.

'Are you jealous?'

'What's jealous?'

'Do you want all the good things for yourself?' Then she was sorry she said it. She knew, if he could, he would answer he wanted good for her, too. 'Put on an apron. Bring me an egg.'

When Stephen came down, she left the pancake batter settling and brought them each a cup of coffee to drink on the couch. 'Good morning?'

'I'm happy,' he said.

Bill flew across the room, loose apron like a cape wild behind him, dropped between them, half on her lap, the coffee sloshing out of their cups.

'Bill the Pill!'

Then he leapt up and charged again. Nan put out her bare foot to stop him. Gripping her heel, he closed his lips around her big toe and suckled noisily.

'That's silly. Go turn on the stove.'

Nude, strutting, he pulled her along with him. At the kitchen door, she glanced over her shoulder at Stephen.

'Why don't you put him in a treadmill and power your house?' he called. 'Or sell tickets? Kindergarten Burlesque.'

Gingerly, she lifted the little brown cakes with the spatula. Bill carried the plate to Stephen at the table, then stood a moment, head bowed, diligently working something in his mouth. A shiny worm of saliva. Clear and viscous it trailed across the pancakes, still clinging to and stretching off his lip as he set the plate down.

Stephen, unflinching, opened the syrup bottle.

They had a hard day after that, Nan and Bill. Bill put his hand over the page she was reading, said, 'Tell me about when I was a baby.'

'You're not a baby. Soon you'll be in grade one.'

The rest of the afternoon he was all anxiety, plaguing her with questions about school, twisting her answers, finally crying and purposely breaking a dish. She put him to bed before Stephen came, left him breathing heavily in dreams, as if his own badness were sitting on his chest.

Already Stephen was talking marriage.

'I don't know yet. Why force me?'

He didn't mean to, he said. If she knew the answer was no, she should say immediately, not keep him on cruelly. She said she hoped he thought more of her than that.

'I can't say the right thing tonight!'

So they vowed silence the rest of the evening, communicated through fingers, mouthed words. She laughed like a girl as he carried her, awkward, colliding with the walls of the stairwell. A picture slipped from its hook and crashed to the floor, this seeming so wildly funny they could barely stagger into the bedroom. He heaved her into the air and she fell giggling onto the bed, right onto Bill, who shrieked with the whole force of his savage throat.

Stephen found the light switch.

'I'm broken!' Bill wailed.

She was furious. 'One, two, three, into your own room.'

Stephen took each ankle and dragged Bill off the bed, held him a moment upside down while he thrashed like a landed fish.

Crawling between sheets, Nan tried to ignore the deadened thudding of her child hurling himself against the adjoining wall. Relentless shrieking, hysterical waves of fury, and now and then a lull so she thought, thank God, but it was only his coming up for air. Finally she sat up.

Stephen held her back.

'Are you going to tell me not to go to him?'

'No. I just want to say I'm sorry for your trouble.'

Now Lucifer Bill was bucking on the floor. When she touched him, he gave up struggling and clung to her nightgown. 'What?' she asked, lifting his stained face. In the depths of his rage he had forgotten and began to cry again from confusion. She hushed him and brought him to his bed.

'Stephen's mean.'

'He's not mean. He gets frustrated with you and no wonder. You have to get used to Stephen.'

He put his mouth to her ear and breathed the word: mean.

This she promised him, promised herself: if she saw any sign of spite, however small, she would say goodbye to Stephen. She promised easily, half because she did not believe in a child's perception, half because she knew unkindness now would only grow through the years to animosity between two men. Any house divided against itself will not stand.

It was a long time before she left William Lucifer, breath exhausted and clotted, and went back to bed where Stephen, too, had fallen asleep. For her purposes then, she was alone. She lay back, lifted her arms over her head, inhaled, exhaled. The secret addiction of remembering her daughter. She was best indulged seeing Joni as she had been just before the accident, about Bill's age now, when they all realized she was growing into something almost perfect. Patrick had even said, I can't touch her any more, she's too good for me. Hair red and eyes like the whole sky condensed. She had the most elegant carriage of any child and a way of being silent, not shyness – musing – then tipping off some extraordinary thought.

Even now Nan couldn't help thinking Joni was a mistake, that the accident was a way of retrieving something lost from that elsewhere place. As therapy she would imagine the car on that northern highway, afternoon sinking into early dusk. Patrick and Joni in front, her mother in the back with the Christmas cache. They are singing carols and, as in movies, their voices are audible all across the frozen fields, through the wind-breaks of naked trees. Then the truck appears speeding toward them in their own lane. Nothing can be done. In the next image Joni is plucking glass out of the windshield, delicately, though glass could never cut her. She crawls out on the hood of the car, jumps down on a highway brightly littered with coloured parcels. She opens the driver's door and tugs her father's beard, as she always did to tease him, though now it is bloodied. In her green elfin parka, her buckle-up snow boots, Joni is unscathed, but Patrick is unrecognizable. He rises nonetheless. Joni wakes her broken grandmother with a kiss. Picking through the sideways wreckage of the moving van, they find the culpable driver who, even dead, sways from drunkenness. All together they set off cross-country, gore-red trail in the snow, going in the direction of a light behind the trees.

Then Stephen rolled over and she lost her vision. Looking at the fine line of his darkened face, she thought: if Joni were here instead of Bill it would be a different life altogether. A decision would have been taken as spontaneously as a gift. Ease in her day life, night the struggle with the memory of her wayward prodigal son coming back to her as bad as ever, a celebration of his contrariness. And for a time she saw the car, her mother in the back seat, Patrick in the front with William Lucifer, not a toddler but almost six, pulling pieces of foam out of a hole in the seat, putting them in his mouth and spitting them at his grandmother. Patrick is telling him to cut it out when the truck comes barrelling down in their lane.

She sat up with a jerk, put her fist in her mouth to stop her own cry. *She had been thinking of life without Bill. She had been wishing away her only child.* Out of the tangle of covers she kicked, stumbled in the dark. She felt her way to the bathroom, then down the coolness of the toilet tank, urgent, fell forward. She had committed something in her heart, as bad as pushing him down the stairs or locking him out in winter. Her own finger she forced down her throat, stabbed and heaved forward. When Stephen turned on the light she was kneeling on the floor, hands clasped.

She watched from a lawn chair Stephen helping Bill around

the big rocks, into the clear flow of the current. With arms extended, the boy looked like a bony marionette. Over the river noise, Stephen's voice: 'Trust me. Yeah. Trust me.'

Suddenly Bill was back on the shore, running to her.

'What? Don't cling to me! You're wet!'

'Stephen let the water go over my face!'

'It was an accident, I'm sure.'

'Nanny, he pinched my arm!'

She looked at Stephen slogging out of the water. He shook his head and shrugged. 'Put on a T-shirt, Bill. You'll catch cold.'

She returned to her book. She hadn't turned a page yet, but instead was concentrating indulgently on her own bad humour. Perverse, her guilt pushing Bill away instead of bringing him closer. She was conscious of blaming him for the wrong she had done him, and this made her all the more irritable. When she looked up again, he was peeing in the river.

Stephen moved quietly about the picnic site. He set a glass of iced tea next to her without a word to disturb. Later, he took Bill off by the ear to light the coals. She could hear her boy's pugnacious voice shrill across the picnic site and was glad she did not have to be patient with him. Hers was a dire need for silence, silence to fill her life, like the calm she had grown up in. In another minute, Bill was wailing, coming toward her, fist in eye. 'Stephen made the smoke –'

'Bill!' Stephen shouted. 'Leave Nanny alone! She doesn't feel well, can't you see?'

Bill gaped at her, Stephen's scolding red on his face. Nan made a shooing motion with her hand. He hopped up and down on one foot, then scurried off down the river bank.

The ruined myth: each generation betters the preceding. Her mother's grace and wisdom had been lost on her. How she blundered on. What hope was there then for William Lucifer now filling his swimming trunks with river stones?

Her mother would have gotten up and done something, never brooded, sulked. This, and a wasp circling her head, goaded her out of the chair. She took the cloth from the hamper, shook it out over the picnic table, then began to unload the food. Bill came when she was slicing thick slabs of bread. He emptied his swimming trunks, laid fist-sized stones out on the table among the picnic dishes.

Bill's job: transporting the chicken from fire to picnic table. He did this well and took a seat beside her. Stephen loaded the plates with salad.

'Bread please,' said Bill.

'How are you?' Stephen asked her.

'All right. Don't worry.'

'I said bread!'

She thought Stephen was going to shush Bill, but he reached past the basket of bread and picked up a stone. Held it a moment, palm up, as if to learn its weight or significance. Then he put it into Bill's waiting hand, not roughly or even with exasperation, just firmly, communicating. It shocked her more than if he had struck the boy.

Who would set a whole future on the whim of someone else's gesture?

A yellow wasp hovered over the table. She was not afraid. She gave her son a piece of bread.

THE PLANET EARTH

DENISE STARED at Barbara's racked face. Eyes rolled back in counterfeit agony, mouth gaping planet-wide, it belonged on a poster for a B horror movie: *The Swallower*. 'He gets stuck like *that*?' asked Denise.

Barbara was demonstrating how Doug's jaw had locked the night before. Relaxing now into her real face, she explained, 'Subluxation. It happens when he yawns. Can't eat. Can't speak.' She smirked. 'I like him like that.'

'Is it painful?'

'Very.'

Denise got up and went to the counter for the coffee pot. They were in her café. Through the short-order window she could see into the kitchen – the cook humped down in the alley doorway dragging on a cigarette, sunlight on his shoulders; Max unloading the dishwasher, ploddingly, spoon by spoon. She selected the pot with the blue ribbon tied to its handle – decaffeinated. Barbara seemed manic enough already.

'I'm the waitress today,' Denise said, refilling their cups.

'What happened to that girl, the chubby one?'

'Didn't show up.' She took the pot back to the warming plate.

'Why can't Max do the tables?'

Denise glanced again at Max in the kitchen. Bent over the dishwasher, he was a poetic inspiration – *The white moon and its twin...* 'He can't remember the orders.'

'After twenty years?'

'Give him a break. The menu's changed.' Denise sat down and, sipping her coffee, gave her friend a long look. Since the café had opened a few months before, Barbara had been 'dropping by' regularly, taking three different buses in from the suburbs, a journey that seemed to Denise so complicated and exhausting only the truly desperate would embark upon it.

'We're going to get busy soon,' she said.

Alluding like this to the time, Denise knew, was like firing a starting pistol. Barbara, having warmed up with aimless chatter, would now take off with what was really on her mind – her marathon of woes. A month ago her daughter had left for university in Montreal.

'You know, I'm jealous of Patty,' she confessed. 'She's got some little apartment with another girl. It reminds me of when you and I left Hope.'

Barbara raced on; she wanted to escape the house, to get a job, but had lost confidence when she found out that typewriters had become obsolete. 'I'm unqualified, all right! Unqualified for *life!*'

Ten minutes later and still running. She had never learned to drive a car. There were thirty extra pounds unevenly and unflatteringly distributed all over her body, like a winter coat with the pockets stuffed. Finally she bounded across the finish line, neck-and-neck with her worst gripe.

'I just don't want Doug touching me any more. He knows it, too, but last night in bed he pulled that same old trick. He inches closer, as if he can have me if he takes me by surprise.'

'So what did you do?'

Barbara leaned conspiratorially over her coffee cup. 'You know how a yawn is contagious?'

'You made his jaw lock?'

Spontaneously Barbara's and Denise's mouths stretched wide, their eyes crossed ludicrously. *The Swallowers.* Hooting with laughter, they knocked their cups together. For the first time since they had started getting together again it felt like the old Barbara and Denise, best friends.

Barbara took one last swig of coffee, then stood to go.

'How do you fix it, by the way?' asked Denise.

'His jaw? I give him a good smack.'

The week after Denise and Barbara graduated from high school they caught the Greyhound to Vancouver, singing Crosby, Stills, Nash and Young all the way through the valley. Never again would they say, 'I live in Hope.' Or, 'I Hope it doesn't rain.' Nothing in that drizzling town could hold two girls like these, one reasonably brainy, the other with good legs.

Denise was sick of her parents. Sick, sick, sick. It wasn't that they hounded or cramped her. Rather, they left her too much alone, starring in their own little melodrama with Denise as their audience. She booed and cat-called. 'Get a divorce!' were her parting words. As for Barbara, her three older sisters were all pregnant at the same time. When the extended family united for Sunday dinner the vomiting terrified her. She wanted to live a little before that happened to her.

They rented a furnished bachelor suite in Kitsilano, its proximity to the beach compensating for the mildew. 'Furnished' meant a kitchen table, two unmatching chairs and a Murphy bed that pulled out of the wall like a drawer. Opening the bed that first night, they shrieked in disgust; the mattress was a record in blotches of all the previous tenants. Or, as Denise imagined, it was an astigmatic cartographer's projection of the earth – the stains the continents misshapen and askew. South America was obviously blood. Barbara thought menstrual blood; Denise said, 'Somebody picked a cherry.' Neither wanted to lie down on it so they bought a cot and made this rule: the last one home sleeps with Murphy.

Denise didn't show her skinny legs. She wore long tie-dyed skirts and got a job in a café on Fourth Avenue, the Planet Earth, that specialized in vegan cuisine.

'I don't get it,' said Barbara. 'It's called the Planet Earth but you sell food from Venus.' Tofu made her fart so they instituted another rule: Denise couldn't bring any home. Instead she brought her contempt for the clientele of the Planet Earth. 'I am a flower!' she sang, swaying on the Murphy bed, arms swirling around her. 'Feel my good vibrations.' She claimed to despise everyone in Kitsilano except Barbara, Max – bus boy from the Planet Earth – and her boss, Peter, who owned the café but was at the same time a supposedly penniless Hare Krishna distributing the *Bhagavad Gita* downtown in front of the Bay.

Denise also brought home men she met in the café.

'This is Frank. Frank, tell Barb your favourite colour.'

'Psychedelic.'

Another was a Jesus look-alike. 'Come on, Charlie. Sing us a tune from *Godspell*.' Charlie grinned and slapped the patches on his jeans. Later, to be rid of these admirers, Denise told them she had a fiancé named Murphy.

That summer Barbara enrolled in typing and shorthand courses at Pitman's and by fall was working in an insurance office, spending her paycheque on magazines and clothes. She bought a skirt suit made of lime green vinyl and a paper dress. Seemingly she was the opposite of Denise, but somehow they fit together, like the continents had once fit together. And like the continents, they started drifting too. Doug, one of the insurance agents, proposed. After that Barbara was always the last one home, so, in the end, got both the fiancé and Murphy.

Barbara gone and most of the lunch crowd cleared out, Denise sat at the counter picking at her tabouli, watching Max wrangle with a napkin holder at a nearby table. He gripped it – one of those stainless-steel, spring-loaded affairs – and with fumbling, child-like motions inserted a batch of napkins. Then he paused, deliberating, wiping his palms on his jeans.

The real reason she wouldn't let Max wait on tables, Denise was reminded now, was that his jeans were always riding low, the crotch flapping dangerously near his knees. 'Say no to crack, Max!' she told him a hundred times a day. 'Hoist them jeans!' Once she'd bought him a belt, but he lost it.

'How do you lose a belt?' she'd asked.

'I dunno.'

Exasperated, she'd snapped, 'What you don't know could fill a book.' Max beamed. He always took that as a compliment.

Now he turned the holder around and stuffed the empty side with napkins. The opposite side strained, then burst, napkins fanning out across the table. Painstakingly, he gathered and reloaded them. The other side popped again. Denise rolled her eyes. Max's face, however, was unmarred by frustration, placid as an emaciated Buddha's. Conceivably, he could go on like this for the rest of the afternoon.

She dropped her fork. 'Max, come here. I want to talk to you.'

He shuffled over, tugging at his waistband.

'What was the name of that waitress?'

'You mean Judy?' Max asked.

'Right. Why did she quit?'

'I dunno.' He looked at his feet in the yellow canvas basketball sneakers she'd bought him.

'Yes you do.'

'She didn't like working here.'

'Why not?'

'I dunno. You called her Missy. Her name was Judy.'

Denise smiled. Luckily Judy hadn't heard Denise's other name for her, 'Turkey Wattles', a reference to her untoned haunches. 'Do *you* like working here, Max?'

A grin a dentist would love to snap a brace on. 'You bet!'

What else would he have said? He was her hostage. How can he stand it, she wondered. How can he stand me?

Though Denise had been seeing Peter the Hare Krishna monogamously for almost a year, she couldn't bring him to Barbara and Doug's wedding. He wore a spotless white robe; he was supposed to be celibate. Barbara was the only other person who knew the truth about the relationship. Not even Peter suspected monogamy.

'I don't get it,' said Barbara. 'What's in it for you?'

'Good sex,' said Denise. 'I love the feel of his stubbly head on my bare thighs.'

'If you ask me, he's a crook.'

'If you ask me,' said Denise, 'Doug's an insurance salesman.'

She didn't really have anything against Doug. It was just that he was about to bring an end to the best time of her life. No more would she and Barbara drink too much coffee, then sit up half the night on the beach, Denise saying ugly things about other people and unburdening on Barbara her fears for the world. As the wedding date approached, her pain in losing

Barbara grew so acute that only by focusing on the greater agony of the planet could she bear it. She wrote desperate protest letters and had Barbara sign them too. Her arches fell, she marched in so many demonstrations wearing buffalo sandals. Back in Hope the night before the wedding, her despair reached its nadir. 'Neither of us is going to see thirty, do you realize that?! This planet is doomed! So tell me ... what's the point of getting married?' They held each other, sobbing until dawn, so when the wedding photos came back Barbara was dubbed 'The Bloodshot Bride'.

Years later Patty was going through the photo album, selecting pictures to take with her to Montreal. 'Were you stoned when you married Dad?'

Barbara pulled a wry face. 'I wish I had such a good excuse.' Truly, she couldn't recall her reasons other than he was a good dancer and her sisters had all married by age twenty.

In another picture Denise, maid of honour, peace signs dangling from her ears, glowered into the camera like a doomsayer. Days after that photo was taken Peter absconded to India without a word. Denise quit the Planet Earth. She quit monogamy. With a part-time job proof-reading for a publisher, she paid her way through university.

She saw thirty after all. In fact, Denise saw thirty-nine. That winter her father telephoned from Hope. Usually he cupped his hand over the receiver and browbeat her mother in the background even before he said hello. This time he exchanged a few griping comments with her about the rain, then informed her that her mother had passed away.

Denise was not particularly surprised. As far as she was concerned her mother had ever been the melodramatic maiden tied to the tracks of life. The train barrelling down on her, its cow-catcher gleaming, was not just cancer, but life itself. What shocked Denise much more, what left her standing flabbergasted before the open casket, was the bequest. In itself it meant nothing. Her mother had left her a fair amount of money, as parents do everywhere without repenting in the least their lack of interest in their children. The point was

Denise had always assumed financial dependency had cast her mother in a Punch and Judy marriage. Now it turned out that she had played the role by choice.

At the funeral Denise gazed around at the other mourners. Apart from Barbara, they could have been members of the Hope Amateur Theatrical Society for all she knew. Then her father, seated next to her, did something entirely out of character. He began to weep. He hid his face in his bully hands and quaked with sobs. 'Alma, Alma, Alma...' he gurgled. In all her life Denise had never heard him call her mother anything but 'Dopey'. So they had loved each other after all. What had seemed a drama of domestic failure had really been a tragicomedy of commitment. All those years in a front row seat, Denise hadn't seen it.

Later, at home, Denise dropped her black dress in a circle round her feet. Staring down, it occurred to her that she'd lived her whole life like that – ringed by blackness. She kicked the dress aside, stripped and stood naked before the mirror. For the first time she saw herself as almost middle-aged, saw how slender had made way for gaunt, blonde for an adulterated shade. She saw a curled lip. A woman alone.

Barbara telephoned a few days later. Although Denise was Patty's godmother, work had been so hectic she hadn't seen either Barbara or Patty in several years. 'Freelance editor,' Denise's card announced. 'Freelance dating,' she sometimes wrote on the back before handing it to a man. She didn't have a lot of time to mess around.

'I wanted to check up on you,' said Barbara. 'Are you okay?'

'I'm fine. Thanks.' Then, 'Barb, do you remember the Planet Earth?'

'I live on it.'

'I bought it,' said Denise.

The man Denise was freelance dating at the time was a book illustrator. While she haggled on the phone with the organic produce distributor and the free-range poultry farm, he painted the earth on the café window. He patched it with deserts and oceans, then, peering through a magnifying glass, daubed in rain forests and mountains, finally suspending it all in a blue net bag of rivers. Even before the café opened, people stood on the sidewalk outside enraptured by the genesis.

The Vancouver Sun published an article about the rebirth of the Planet Earth. Twenty years ago the café was the counter-culture hangout. Now, with its unbleached paper napkins and organic espresso beans, nostalgic former flower-children could share a booth with the nouveau environmentally aware.

'This place is politically correct,' said the illustrator. 'You're going to make a pile.'

'That's not what I'm after,' said Denise. 'I used to care about the world.'

She told Barbara, too, about her renewed concern for the planet, but Barbara had only half-run her marathon of woes. 'The worst thing about Doug is he always plays it safe.'

'He's an insurance salesman,' said Denise.

'He's a manager. What I mean is he won't take a chance. He knows our marriage is in trouble, but he won't do anything about it. He's just waiting to see what I'll do.'

Since her mother's death, Denise had been thinking seriously of monogamy. She'd broken off with the book illustrator, torn pages of telephone numbers from her Filofax, eliminated from her life all the men who weren't interested in commitment. Then she discovered she didn't know any men interested in commitment. 'Do you think Doug has always been faithful?'

'Sure. It's not safe to fool around.'

'Must be great,' said Denise.

'You mean AIDS? I don't care. I wish someone else would take him for a roll.' Barbara leaned over her coffee cup. 'Do you think I should divorce him?'

'Do you think I should get married?' asked Denise.

Later she posed the same question to Max. He laughed.

'What's so funny?'

'I'm a bachelor for sure.'

'I didn't mean marry *you*, you idiot!'

If Barbara wanted out of her marriage, Denise figured she would relieve her friend by stepping right into it herself. She called Doug at his office and asked if, in his opinion, her life was worth insuring. He said he'd come round the next day with the forms.

He stood in her bedroom, bare knees clacking above his argyle socks. 'It makes it easier to do this knowing you're a friend of Barbara's.' He meant either that Denise was less likely to kiss and tell, or that he valued their mutual esteem for his wife. 'Doug,' said Denise, preferring the latter interpretation, 'I admire your devotion.'

A month later, when Doug showed no signs of transferring his devotion from Barbara to her, Denise insisted they meet at Barbara and Doug's house. Barbara, after taking a course in word processing, had recently started working for a temp agency; potentially she could come home at any moment. Denise didn't know, however, that the house was wired to Maximum Security standards, that if anyone so much as set foot on the driveway, the alarm would sound, giving them ample time to dress and escape by the back door. There was even, Denise was appalled to discover, a television monitor in the bedroom.

'This isn't a house!' she cried. 'It's a fortress!' She was afraid to get into bed first, in case it was booby-trapped.

Barbara, meanwhile, continued dropping by the Planet Earth a couple of times a week to harp on her stalemate with Doug. Then Denise got a perplexed Doug to take the sheets off the bed so they could make love on the bare mattress.

'Do you remember the Murphy bed we had in Kitsilano?' Denise asked the next day.

'Vaguely,' said Barbara.

Now, with Doug in the shower, Denise wandered naked around the bedroom. Doug, she realized, was never going to confront Barbara. But this, after all, was why she wanted him, for his loyalty, for the cufflinks awarded to him for twenty faithful years in insurance. Denise's own hints to Barbara had proved too subtle. She opened the closet, found Barbara's wardrobe fastidiously organized – blouses arm in arm with other blouses, dresses and skirts and slacks with their kin. Then she began changing their order, breaking up the tidy garment families. She crossed to the dresser, opened a drawer and stirred up Barbara's lingerie.

On top of the dresser was the tortoiseshell vanity set Barbara had brought from Hope. Denise picked up the brush and drew it through her hair, studying herself in the mirror – navel, hip bones like handles, the wiry black diamond of pubic hair. Laying down the brush, she toyed a moment with the manicure kit, then flipped open the jewellery box. The year they lived together, she'd given Barbara a pendant for her birthday. There it was, a silver-plated peace sign, slightly dinted where Patty had teethed on it as an infant. It reminded Denise that she'd never had another friend like Barbara, nor a lover whom she would have chosen over the Barbara of twenty years ago. Ironically, she knew if roles had been reversed back then, she wouldn't even have traded Barbara for Doug.

In the mirror, she saw herself holding up the little manicure scissors and frowning. Then she began, with tiny precise snips, to cut away at her pubic hair. Like a Brillo pad it came off, like a baby rat in her hand. Carefully, she nestled it in Barbara's jewellery box and closed the lid.

Doug said he didn't even like Denise. The affair had been purely sexual. Barbara, after all, had held back on him for so long. 'I don't want to be alone,' he told her.

'I don't blame you,' said Barbara, packing her suitcase. 'I don't want to be alone with you either.'

Apparently Denise did; a week later she moved in with Doug.

To give herself time to think, Barbara flew to Montreal to visit Patty. Unfortunately, it turned out to be exam period for the girls. Patty was also surprisingly dispassionate about the separation. First she wanted to know if a divorced Barbara and Doug would continue paying her tuition fees, then how long Barbara intended on crowding her and her roommate out of their apartment. Still, Barbara was reluctant to call Patty selfish. She remembered her own mother visiting from Hope.

Afterward she and Denise had sprawled giggling on the Murphy bed. 'Barbie,' said Denise in Barbara's mother's voice, 'promise you won't bring home any boys.'

Now Barbara had reached the lowest point in a woman's life, the point where she realizes that if she could live her life all over again, she would do it exactly as her mother had told her. She had brought a boy home, even married him. And though until now her main complaint against Doug had been his subluxation and the way everything about him was both insured and assured, she'd always sensed he was soulless.

Denise had a soul. Like a creature from a cheap horror movie it rose from the tar pit of her being, oozing blackness. Barbara was the compassionate heroine, unafraid to approach it. Because she had glimpsed beneath that slimy coating, she could forgive Denise. She knew the monstrous contradiction that pulsed there, like in Denise's relationship with Max. Denise had searched him out after almost twenty years, found him living in the Cobalt Hotel, maybe eating out of garbage cans. What Denise hadn't told Barbara: she paid for his room above the café, fed him, bought his clothes. Barbara had learned that from Max, and from Doug that Max was named as beneficiary on Denise's life insurance policy. In the café, complaints against Max were not tolerated, yet – here was the irony – she hectored and browbeat him all day long herself. So, after the initial shock, what Denise had left in Barbara's jewellery box seemed less an insult, more like when Denise had flattened her arches to get the u.s. out of Vietnam: self-sacrifice or even a simple favour.

During Denise's years in university, Barbara had been trying her best to stay supine so that she might carry one of her pregnancies to term. They saw each other occasionally, but more often talked on the phone. After Patty was born, Barbara and Doug moved out to the suburbs; they might as well have moved off the planet. Soon Barbara picked up other friends, mostly women with whom she discussed child-rearing, she'd been so relieved at finally producing a daughter.

The earth rotates. It revolves around the sun. This makes time which supposedly goes only forward. Now Barbara wanted it to go back, even felt beneath her feet the planet grinding to a halt, then gearing up again in the opposite direction. Her proof: all around the world trends were reversing – in politics and fashion and attitude. When twenty years ago came completely round again, Barbara was going to go and see Denise. Meanwhile, she intended to get her life on a different track.

Back from Montreal, she rented a tiny apartment near the ocean. That winter reminded her of Hope, the lustreless sky and cold unceasing drizzle. Days the temp agency didn't call she spent on the beach in her rubber boots and anorak, huddled on a driftwood log, grateful at last for her thirty extra pounds of insulation. She was watching the freighters on the bay, stationary against the doleful grey backdrop of mountains, hugely patient, waiting their turn to move into the harbour. When they did finally go, their choreography – profoundly dignified – gave Barbara a reassurance equal to the volume of water they displaced. If someone could manoeuvre those enormous vessels, then she could drive a car, and if she could drive a car, she could steer her life. She knew it. It gave her hope.

The boy was wearing a tie-dyed T-shirt. 'That's what we wore when I was your age,' Barbara told him.

'Far out,' he said.

Barbara circled the car, a green Toyota hatchback seemingly patched together with bumper stickers. NO NUKES. ONE NUCLEAR BOMB CAN RUIN YOUR WHOLE DAY. ARMS ARE FOR HUGGING.

'You can get those off easy. I'll do it for you. They're obsolete now anyway.'

'That's okay,' said Barbara. 'I like them.'

'Wanna take her for a spin?' He banged on the hood.

'I can't drive,' said Barbara.

So he chauffeured her around Kitsilano, up and down the gentrified streets, past the Planet Earth. 'Have you ever eaten there?' asked Barbara

'Too expensive.'

Then he parked the car in front of her apartment building and waited while Barbara counted out four hundred dollars. He hesitated with the money in his hand.

'You saw it's a standard?'

'That's what I want.'

Even after Patty had begun school, Doug had continued to discourage Barbara from learning to drive. He'd argued she would increase the cost of their insurance. Only at her insistence did he take her to the mall parking lot after hours and let her get behind the wheel. 'Ig-ni-tion!' he bellowed. 'Re-verse!'

Driving school was less like the army. Carl, her instructor, truly seemed to want Barbara to learn how to drive. She sensed his yearning every time she stepped on the accelerator. After her first week's lessons, Barbara went out and sat in her Toyota, just to get the feel of it. The next day she asked Carl about the third pedal, discovered a 'standard' transmission was not in fact 'regular'. They laughed about that as they changed cars, but then the learning became more difficult. Co-ordinating the clutch and the gears seemed to Barbara a lot like patting her head and rubbing her stomach at the same time. Still, she persevered.

Several weeks later the telephone woke her. The glowing digits on the clock, 2:37, ruled out the temp agency. Patty was in Cuba for spring break. Barbara lifted the receiver to a familiar caterwauling.

'It's *The Return of the Swallower*,' said Denise. 'What the hell is he saying?'

Doug's agony sounded directly in the phone. 'Auughh! Auu-ggg-hh!'

'That's his love call,' said Barbara.

'Very funny. What am I supposed to do?'

'I bought a car.'

'I thought you couldn't drive,' said Denise.

'I'm taking lessons.'

'Good for you. This place is way the hell out. I never realized it before. How could you stand it without a car?'

'I'm not there any more,' said Barbara.

'Right.' Denise paused. 'Should I take Doug to the hospital?'

'He won't go. They give him a muscle relaxant. He hates needles.'

'He's in pain, Barb.'

Something she'd been thinking about: 'Do you remember when we lived in Kits, the time someone stole our panties out of the laundry room?'

'What?'

'You remember. The next morning we left for work and found them hanging off the antennas of the cars parked all along the street.'

'I didn't wear panties,' said Denise.

Barbara started to laugh. 'I miss you, you know. I've been missing you for years.'

Denise was quiet for a moment. Then, in the background, 'Auuggh! Auuggh!'

'What about Doug?' she asked.

'Oh, yeah. On the left side, just by his ear. Hit him hard. *Really hard* or you'll just have to hit him again.'

That was the year swords were beaten into ploughshares, walls unbuilt, tyrants sent scampering, yet close to home petty vandals loitered in idealistic places converting coffee spoons into weapons: someone had been scraping the paint off the Planet Earth. Denise first noticed it unlocking the café door the next morning. Tracts of the southern hemisphere had been reduced to a transparent void and the ocean was polluted with initials. She stalked into the kitchen, grabbed her apron, stopped. For the first time since the Planet Earth had re-opened, the coffee wasn't ready when she arrived.

Immediately she went upstairs. Max never locked his door. She opened it without knocking, saw his monk's cell of a room, the twin bed made tight enough to have been gift-wrapped. She couldn't tell if he'd slept in it and made it, or not gone to bed at all.

Back downstairs, she started on the coffee herself. Scooping the grounds into the filters, her hands shook. She recalled how she'd found Max last year. First she'd located the cook from the old Planet Earth, now head chef in a downtown hotel. He remembered Max all right, but didn't know what had happened to him after the café had closed.

'What about Peter the Bald? Ran into him a few months back. He sells New Age computer programmes. He wears a ponytail.' Then he gave her the name of a post-Denise waitress who'd also had a soft spot for the bus boy. She suggested Denise try the welfare hotels.

The desk clerk at the Cobalt wouldn't look at her, he was so intent on his work: peeling off from the edges inward a huge rusty scab on his arm. 'Is it raining?' he asked. 'Try the Sky Train station on Terminal Ave.'

She climbed the concrete stairs to the platform, saw him saluting trains as they went by. When she sat down next to him, he turned and, as if twenty years had never happened, greeted her. 'Oh, hi ya, Denise.' Over an hour they spent reminiscing; in the end Denise wasn't sure herself if she believed in time.

He scratched continuously at his groin.

'You stink, Max. When did you last have a bath?'

'I dunno.' He grinned and shrugged.

He said he wouldn't mind working again at the Planet Earth, so together they walked the two blocks back to the hotel. GIRLS-GIRLS-GIRLS, the sign read. Denise parked in the back alley and waited for Max to come down with his suitcase. A star-shaped nipple pastie was lying in the road. From the rim of the overflowing dumpster, a crow swooped down and caught it in its beak. Denise began to shake, first her hands, then a seismic tremor through her body. Bringing Max back was her self-reckoning. If the Cobalt Hotel, its curtains patterned in cigarette burns, its hypodermic needles in the toilet – if that ever lured him back, it would be a measure of herself and the Planet Earth.

She lifted the first filter into the coffee maker, let slip one side, spilling grounds in the machine and on the counter. 'Shit!'

'...happy and you know it clap your hands...'

With her forearm, she swept the grounds onto the floor. She turned the whole machine upside-down and dropped it in the sink. Then she heard him.

'*... and you really want to show it...*'

Following his tuneless warble out of the kitchen, through the café, she was led right to the door of the men's room.

'*... stamp your feet...*'

'Coffee, Max!' She rapped hard. 'Coffee!'

'Help!' he cawed. 'Let me out!'

He'd been trapped in there all night, he told Denise after she popped the lock with a kebab skewer. He'd slept sitting on the toilet, leaning into the wall. Denise didn't know whether to run him through with the skewer or embrace him. The early morning sunlight coming through the window cast a blue and green pool in the middle of the café. It was the swirling chaos the world had begun in, where it would end eventually. She put her arm around his shoulder and walked him to the kitchen.

'Do you know what an adulterer is, Max?'

He squinted, shaking his head.

'It's someone pretending to be an adult.'

'You sure know a lot, Denise.'

'What I don't know could fill a book.'

'That's for sure.'

'Pull up your pants.'

Clutch pressed, gear shifted, now Barbara was skimming down the highway, dizzy with the triumph of coming this far. Though her eyes were immovably fixed on the asphalt ahead of her, in her peripheral vision the exit signs reared, then vanished in the dark. What she would do when she reached her own exit was theoretical; very likely she would shoot past it and end up back in Hope.

A vehicle approached from the fast lane, drove along beside her for a moment, then honked. Panicking, Barbara clutched tighter to the wheel, raised her foot, and the instant she broke contact with the pedal, fell victim to New Driver's Amnesia: she couldn't remember which pedal was the accelerator, which the brake. Coursing along, suspended, she perceived from the corner of her eye the other vehicle still escorting her. Honk. She was losing speed. Honk. Finally she turned her

head, saw with immense relief not a police cruiser, but a battered pick-up. The driver, a young man, pointed to her
antenna, gesticulated lewdly and sped off.

Barbara laughed. Suddenly she felt bolstered by her own
recklessness. She was driving uninsured. Furthermore, having
failed to earn her licence, she was free from the strictures of
the Department of Motor Vehicles. Her error: she had parallel
parked with one wheel on the curb. 'You left the road!' Carl
had told her, tears brimming in his eyes. Now her exit was
immediately before her. Instinctively, she found the accelerator. Daringly, she took the curve. At that speed, she seemed to
lift right off the highway and cut the corner in the air. Then
she was soaring above the overpass, swooping low over the
dark roofs of the suburb, the sparkling grid of street lights, in
her mind – flying, riding the night sky.

When Barbara touched down on Denise and Doug's driveway, the alarm sounded first, then the crash. Denise, coinci-
dentally, hadn't been asleep, but staring at the silver glow off
the television monitor thinking about Barbara, so when Doug
fired the remote control and the screen bloomed to a picture of
the car that had just rammed into their garage door, Denise
knew instantly it was Barbara, just as if memory, not the car,
had transported her.

'What the hell?' Doug said.

Denise, palms over her ears to shut out the scream of the
alarm, stared at the screen in amazement. The car, stalled in
reverse at the end of the driveway, had a pair of panties hanging off the aerial. When it lurched forward again the panties
were buoyed aloft with the force of the acceleration. For a second they seemed to spread out, majestically, a sail full of air.
Then impact – another very big bang – the beginning or the
end of the world.

'Doug,' Denise said. 'Let's show Barb how we unlocked your
jaw last night.' She poured coffee into his cup, then Barbara's.

'No,' said Doug peevishly.

'It was like something you'd see on "Championship Wres-
tling". I really had to whale on him. Didn't I, Doug?'

'I'm going to bed,' he announced, pushing his cup aside and standing.

'Okay, honey,' said Denise. 'We'll join you in a minute.'

Barbara's crying was now ambiguously half-laughter. Denise tossed her the panties to blow her nose in. Barbara waved them at Doug as he stalked out of the kitchen.

'What I remember about those panties on the aerials,' said Denise, sitting down at the table, 'was how they reminded me of pictures I'd seen of the United Nations.' Except that all the countries of the world waved an identical pure white flag. She remembered being eighteen and idealistic and walking down that avenue of banners arm in arm with Barbara. 'Also, I had to work in the café all day long, in a skirt, without any underwear!'

'We didn't own any any more!' cried Barbara. 'We were *so free!*'

Denise tapped the rim of her cup as she took a sip. 'This ain't decaff, by the way. We're going to be up all night.'

AND THE CHILDREN SHALL RISE

HE WATCHES her small thin fingers, quick like animals, scrabbling, as they crouch together on the side of the road.

'Help me,' she says.

He obeys, running his hand along the curb base until he strikes a pebble.

'Here.' He smiles.

She takes the pebble and puts it in its place, her only acknowledgement acceptance, although he waits for a word.

'Give me that one.' She points to a rock nearby. He needs two hands to lift it. He is only four.

'More little ones,' she says.

Soon the circle of stones is closed. He places his palm in the centre, but she grabs his wrist and yanks him away. She leans forward, hair brushing the ground, then spits where his hand was. From her blouse pocket she takes a matchbox and holds it out to him. She shakes it; the sound is not matches.

'What's in there?' he asks.

Carefully, solemnly, she opens the little drawer.

'Caterpillars,' he says.

She nods.

'Caterpillars! Caterpillars! Where did you find them?'

'Watch,' she says.

She takes a caterpillar from the box and puts it in the centre of the circle, on the dark mark of her saliva. A beautiful thing, it is peacock and starred and fringed with fine hairs. It crawls away. With her finger she guides it back to the centre. He reaches out to play too, but she stops his hand again. Then, quickly, so quickly he sees only the fleeting blur of her arm, the arc of a movement, she slams the rock down.

He stares at her. After a moment she turns her face, squinting as if the sun is in her eyes, and lifts the rock. In the circle of stones is a jellied mass, green and yellow, glistening.

'Is it dead?' he asks.

'Yes. Do you want to do it?'

'No.'

'Then you pick one.'

He selects a caterpillar, then watches the stone crush it.

'What are you doing, Carol?'

They look up. His mother is standing over them.

'Nothing,' Carol says.

'It's not nothing,' says his mother. 'You're killing things.' She crouches too. 'Look, poor caterpillars. How do you think they feel?'

'Dead,' says the boy.

'How do you think they feel?' she asks Carol.

'How do you think I feel?' Carol replies.

He watches his friend walk away down the road. She has long black hair past her waist and a step that is smooth and careless. Barefoot, she moves as if she has her whole life to get to where she is going. She stops and bends, scratches her ankle, then walks on with her arms out from her sides like wings.

'It's not that I don't like Carol Bell,' his mother says later.

'I like Carol Bell,' he says.

'I like her too. But she's seven, you know.'

'I'm four,' he says.

'I know. That's what I'm saying, Philip. You are four and she is seven.'

'You are a hundred,' he says.

She laughs and kisses him. 'I'm sorry there aren't other children your age here. Do you miss your friends?'

'I miss Daddy.'

'Yes,' she says. 'Sometimes I do too, though I shouldn't.'

They have left his father behind and come to this little house in this summer town, where the roads are always dusty and no one wears shoes. His mother is painting again now.

'I like Carol Bell,' he says.

'Yes, she has beautiful hair.'

He is playing on the swings with Carol Bell. She swings high, then leans back so her hair sweeps the grass. He tries to do the same, but falls backward with a thump.

She peers down at him. 'Do you want a push?'

'No.'

Carol Bell has pushed him before, slammed her hands against his back and sent him to dizzy, terrifying heights. He called for her to stop, pleaded for her to stop, and when she finally did, she ran away. He does not want her to run away now.

'Let's sit sideways then,' she says.

He gets up and they straddle the swings, facing each other. Carol sways back and forth, gazing up at the sky. Her eyes are dark and deep-set, ringed with a faint blueness like smoke. Without looking at him, she glides forward and knocks her swing against his.

'Don't,' he says.

She knocks him again.

'Please don't.'

Then she smiles, just slightly, turning up the corners of her mouth and making her lips look smooth like fruit skin. She smashes into his swing with such force that between his legs there is only a sharp, singing pain. His face crumples. He is going to cry.

'I'm hungry,' she says quickly. 'Go get us something to eat.' She takes his arm and shakes it. 'Get something to eat.'

By the time he is in the kitchen, his hand between his legs, he no longer needs to cry. He comes back with carrot sticks in one hand, his mother holding the other. 'She'll only give us carrots,' he tells Carol.

She plucks one from his fist.

'Don't you get breakfast, Carol?' his mother asks.

'Yes.'

'What did you have for breakfast this morning?'

'Pancakes with blueberries and strawberries. And coffee,' Carol says.

'Coffee?'

'Yes. I always drink coffee. I like it.'

'Do you want to have lunch here?' his mother asks.

'Yes.' Carol takes another carrot stick.

At lunch his mother asks after Carol's mother. Carol says that her mother is dead.

'What?' his mother exclaims. Then she frowns. 'You're not telling the truth. I met your mother. And just the other day I saw her drive by.'

'It wasn't my mother.'

'Yes, it was. She waved to me.'

'Anyway,' says Carol Bell, 'my brother is always screaming because of it.'

The boy stares at her with his mouth hanging open, showing his half-chewed sandwich.

'Carol,' says his mother, 'I don't think you're telling the truth.'

'I am,' she says. 'He sounds like this.' She throws back her head and screams.

The boy looks at his mother unhappily.

'Well, we hope that your brother will be all right,' she says. Then, slyly, 'Here's a cup of coffee for you. What do you take in it, Carol?'

'Nothing. I drink it black.'

And she does. She drinks it down black as if it were chocolate. His mother puts her hand over her mouth. She knows better than to test Carol Bell, or the boy's father, or anyone.

There is just the boy and his mother living together in the small house, warm and close.

'Two buns in a basket,' she tells him, beginning their game.

'Two bugs in a rug,' he says.

'Two birds in a nest.'

'Two pigs in a pen.'

They fall down laughing and snorting like pigs. There is a love in this laughter that clings like burrs. But the boy wets his bed at night and sometimes cries for no reason.

In the evening when he bathes she sits on the edge of the tub and sings all the songs he asks for – 'Froggie Went A' Courting,' 'Little White Duck,' 'Suzanna's A Funny Old Man.' She takes up the wash cloth but he always wriggles from her embrace.

'Dirty thing,' she teases.

When he is in bed, she reads to him, not more than three, four, stories, then he must brush her hair the hundred strokes. He falls asleep before forty.

'One. Some people lie,' she tells him as he draws the brush through her hair. It is shoulder-length and greying.

'I don't lie,' he says.

'Two. Of course not. You would never lie. Ouch. Daddy lied.'

'No.'

'Three. Yes, and sometimes Carol Bell lies. I want you to know that. Four.'

'Okay.'

'And don't play with Carol Bell except in our yard. Five. All right, Philip?'

They are almost in the yard, just at the end of the driveway, on the road. They have collected sticks, handfuls of dried leaves and grass, bits of paper, and put it all in the circle of stones. Carol takes out the matchbox and shakes it. The sound is matches.

At first there is just smoke, a brown veil that catches on his face, makes his eyes tear. He remembers what his mother told him: smoke follows a liar. He gets up and stands behind Carol. She arranges and rearranges the debris, blows on it, mumbles quietly in sing-song. The pile ignites in a sudden burst of flame. She pulls her hand away and he sees that her finger is burnt. He wonders if she will cry and leans around to look at her face.

'You got hurt,' he tells her.

'What?'

'You got burnt.'

'No, I didn't,' she says.

'You did. Look.'

'I didn't.'

She pulls a stick out of the little fire and waves it around in the air. The flaming end makes a glowing baton. The boy, seeing the circles and figure-eights she is drawing, laughs.

'Watch,' she says.

She takes the end of her hair and touches the fire stick to it. He hears the sizzle, smells the stench. 'That's awful,' he says. She laughs.

Other days they build other fires, in the yard now, under the willow where they are hidden by the curtain of leaves, next to the swing set, on the walk. His mother catches them when the fire spreads to a dry patch on the lawn. She rushes out of the house with a doormat and beats the fire into the ground, but a star-shaped singe remains, a reminder. The mat is ruined. The boy stands by with his finger in his mouth. Carol Bell is gone.

Their city house was large with windows even in the ceiling, a fireplace, a spiral stair. His father is an artist too. Sometimes the boy was allowed to play in his father's studio. The paintings were huge, almost the size of the studio wall, bright as balloons and puzzling. In some smaller paintings the boy could recognize a subject, usually a person, but only because his mother pointed it out to him, saying, 'Look. Who do you think she is?' and never answering when he said, 'I don't know.'

Now in this new town, this small house, his mother works all day. She paints him as he plays and later he laughs at the border of gold she always draws around his body. She bought him a bamboo cage and two finches, then painted the birds preening a plumage that was not theirs at all, too vivid, shocking. When she does not paint, she cooks and bakes, changes his sour wet sheets in the dark, kisses him. She throws down her brushes.

'I have hardly worked in four years. Now I have all the time I need. So what's wrong with me?' She says this aloud but, the boy knows, not to him.

He sits on the front step with Carol Bell. She stretches her thin legs in the sun. Her feet are astonishingly dirty, the soles black, toenails encrusted. He has never seen her wearing shoes. While she speaks, he fidgets nervously. She says that everyone in her family has a disease; her sister was sent to where they put crazy people.

'Where do they put crazy people?' he asks.

'Far away. Another country, I think. They tie her to a chair.'

Her mother coughs ceaselessly. 'Sometimes blood comes out, sometimes green stuff, sometimes spiders.'

He cringes. 'Spiders!'

The boy does not know what to say about these horrors, so he says nothing. Then she gets up and walks to the middle of the lawn. She raises her arms in the air and lifts one leg so she is posed in a crude arabesque. The sun is on her back. He watches and waits for her next movement.

She does not stir for such a long time that he is just about to call to her. Suddenly her arms stretch wide and her hair comes alive, fanning and spreading into a wheel. He watches her, open-mouthed, watches and is dizzied. Minutes before she frightened him; now she mystifies, turns and turns, a bit of paper trapped in a wind eddy, and he is sure that she will rise up from the lawn and spin away. Seeing her prepare for flight, he kicks off his sandals and runs onto the lawn.

The moment he joins her, she stops. Embarrassed, he goes back to the step and struggles to rebuckle his sandals. Carol Bell, meanwhile, begins walking along the edge of the flower bed. From the corner of his eye, he sees her crouching. When he finally looks up, though, she has disappeared.

'Gone home,' he says unhappily.

He shuffles over to the flower bed to see if she has left a print of her bare feet. He sees instead that Carol Bell has pulled the heads off all the flowers.

'Did Carol Bell do this?' his mother asks.

'No,' he answers.

'No? Who did it then? Philip, who did it?'

'Me,' he tells her.

'You? Oh, Philip, don't say that. I know it's not true.' He looks at her and notices a streak of blue paint across her cheek. 'Did Carol do it?'

'No. Me.'

She sighs and takes his hand. 'Now what am I supposed to

do with you? Listen, Philip, if I catch Carol Bell at this sort of thing again, I'll go to her mother.'

'Her mother has a disease,' he says.

'Nonsense. Carol Bell tells stories. Carol Bell lies.'

He says, 'I like Carol Bell.'

She covers the paint streak on her face with her hand, as if it pains her.

The boy brings a tumbler of water from the house and takes it to Carol Bell who sits at the end of the driveway. He is conscious of his mother standing in the front window watching, the way she used to watch his father. Carol grips a stick between her knees and works at fraying the end, but her fingernails are too bitten down; finally she uses her teeth.

They have made a volcano, swept the dust off the road to shape a hill, then pushed a finger down through the top. Carol carefully pours water into the hole. Then she stirs with the frayed stick, adds more water to make a thin batter. 'Paint,' she tells him. He claps his hands in glee.

She bites her lip, showing small teeth, and her face twists with the strain of concentration. She begins painting in mud on the driveway.

'Do a boat!' he says, but she is not listening.

Soon her strokes steady. With each line he tries to guess her picture and hopes it will be a boat. He thinks that she, seven years old, must be a fine artist and capable of drawing a fine boat. Then his face falls. She is not drawing but writing. He cannot read.

He sits in silent disappointment. She appears to be writing a painfully long word. Bored, he looks up and waves to his mother at the window. She disappears and a moment later is walking down the driveway toward them, arms crossed, frowning. Carol continues writing.

In one motion his mother swoops down, tears the stick out of Carol Bell's hand and hoists her up by the arm. She shouts, 'You wash that! Do you hear me? Wash it and never do it again!'

'What does it say?' asks the boy.

'Another thing. I'm going to talk to your mother. I'm tired of your pranks.'

Carol Bell stands stiffly and allows herself to be shaken. He has never seen the girl frightened before. Now she stares at his mother with wide eyes. His mother's expression softens and reddens to a fluster.

'I have to tell your mother.'

Carol's face stretches into a grimace. He thinks she will cry, but she just stands there with her terrible twisted face, then jerks her arm free. He watches her walk slowly down the road, rubbing her arm.

'Get the hose, please, Philip.'

'What does it say?'

'Nothing.'

He is brushing her hair. A finch died that afternoon and they are both saddened though he could not accept her comfort. They forget to count his strokes. She tells him that the bird was good and will certainly go to heaven. He asks her if Carol Bell will go to heaven.

'Oh, Philip. I feel sorry for the girl, poor pretty thing. That lovely hair, those filthy feet. But with her lying, her mischief, she's a bad influence on you. I should have talked to Mrs. Bell and not gone back on my word. But the look on her face! How could I?'

'Will you go to heaven?' he asks.

She turns to him. 'What do you think?'

He is not sure, so he shrugs. Then he says, 'If Daddy goes with you.'

She breathes deeply, making a noise like wind to clear away his blame.

Carol Bell is gone for several days and the boy misses her. He lingers at the front of the house, on the lawn where she once did her dance, down at the end of the driveway where they had their circle of stones. When at last he resigns himself to her absence, she appears, beckoning to him from behind the hedge. He goes to her delighted, stays the morning, but when he comes into the house for lunch, he is distraught.

He has trouble with his meal. He keeps his right hand under the table.

His mother laughs. 'Is it a game?'

'What?'

'Eating like that. Are you playing a game?'

'Yes,' he says and looks away. When he looks back, she is frowning.

'What's wrong, Philip?'

He begins to cry.

'Give me your hand. Oh, Philip!'

Carol Bell has carved a little figure across the back of his hand. It is not deep, and it did not hurt too much. He likes it, in fact: a strange mark, like a flower or a star, coloured rust with his dried blood.

'Come with me,' she says, 'We're going over there.'

'No!' he cries.

'We must show Carol's mother what Carol did.'

'I'm scared,' he says.

So his mother goes alone, is only gone a few minutes. When she returns she forbids him to play with Carol Bell.

'Carol Bell is on the swings!'

'What?' She comes and looks out the window. 'You stay here. I'll go and talk to her.'

This is the very next day. He can just see her form through the trees. Last night he dreamed of Carol Bell walking away with her arms out from her sides like wings. She spun once around and took to the air. He believed he would never see her again.

'Carol Bell is on the swings!' He follows his mother out the door.

His mother says, 'Carol, what happened?'

'Nothing,' Carol answers.

'What happened to your hair?'

'Nothing.'

'Who cut your hair?'

'Nobody.'

Carol's hair is hacked raggedly, shorter on one side than the other. She swings slowly and smiles at them.

'Did you cut your hair or did your mother cut your hair?'

'No one cut my hair.'

'But it's gone!' cries the boy.

His mother takes him by the hand and leads him into the house again. She sits down on the sofa and stares at the floor.

'Did I make a mistake?' she asks. 'Did I do the wrong thing? What would anyone do?' Then she looks at him, 'Did you know?'

He does not have any answers for her. She holds out her arms and he comes to her, falls forward and touches her cheek. Then he takes her soft skin between his fingers, takes it and twists, pinches with all his strength. She cries out in pain, pushes him away and slaps his face. They look at each other, stunned, stunned by the hate there. Finally he comes again into the circle of her arms and they weep.

GRUNT IF YOU LOVE ME

'HERE HE IS. Only forty-three but with the face of a hard-living man.'

Tina bent to look at her uncle Pat in the back seat of the car. He was about the size of an eight-year-old, most of one freckled fist balled up in his mouth as he rocked back and forth. A Velcro strap secured his glasses. Through the thick lenses, she couldn't tell if he had any eyelashes.

'Look at that nose. Broke eight times.'

'How?'

'He falls down. Don't you, Pat? You're no ballet dancer, are you, Pat? You'll see what I mean when he's out of the car.' Fishing for a cigarette in the pocket of her smock dress, Gran looked Tina up and down. 'You put on weight.'

'I know.'

'Your hair's different.'

'It's a perm.'

'I don't think I like it. It looks like a burning bush.'

'You're just the same, Gran.'

'Three years when you're young and three years when you're old are two different things.' They got in the car. 'Now we gotta take Uncle Pat to day camp. Sunshine Summer Day Camp, right, Pat?' She winked, mock confidentiality. 'Today's his last day, but don't tell him I said so. He gets all choked up when things end.'

At the recreation centre Tina watched Gran unbuckle Pat's seat belt and with a towel wipe away the slobber that wet his whole forearm. Out on the asphalt, he didn't seem able to stand flat-footed, but sprang unsteadily on his toes. Gran pointed to his papery scalp. 'Dandruff. I used to slick him down with Brylcreem, but the flakes showed worse.' Hop, hop, hop. Hop, hop, hop. Dry skin shook loose and fluttered about his shoulders like tiny living moths.

Back home Tina's mother, who hadn't seen her retarded brother in almost twenty years, had prepared Tina by telling her Pat was 'like a child'. An eternal five-year-old, Tina had imagined. A kitten that never grows up. Not an infant in an old man's body, a nose red and mashed down from too many breakings, crooked hands with knuckles like big marbles, drool. The effect of the all-night bus hit her suddenly. 'I'll wait in the car!' She sank low in her seat, staring in the side-mirror at her own reflection pinched tight with disgust.

Tina had come to live with Gran so she could attend a high school with a drama programme. Before long she was a willing recruit for charity. Every Saturday afternoon she shouted herself hoarse, a caller at the Mental Handicap Society Bingo. She solicited five-year light bulbs by telephone. Evenings Gran emptied onto the living-room floor her garbage bag of yarn scraps – crocheting lessons – so Tina, too, might donate her handiwork to the MHS store.

By mid-October, the chain stitch still confounded her.

'You're doing good,' said Gran, 'but try and make the loops more even.'

'I'm trying. I'm trying.'

Gran chuckled. 'So what's playing on Broadway?'

Tina looked up blankly from her tangle of yarn.

'Drama. You came all this way for drama. Are you doing a play?'

'Some stupid thing.'

'What's your part?'

'I'm in the lighting booth.'

And she'd been skulking the halls, binder held like an armour breastplate, hair raked over her eyes to hide a forehead ravaged by pimples. It was those cookies Gran let her make. With a cleaver she hacked big chunks of chocolate off the block. Then, as she put on weight, she rationalized even more cookies: the new high school was so much bigger than the one at home, she would have to expand herself in order to fit in. She thought of the friends who had been jealous of her opportunity. When they called, she lied, told them morosely, 'I'm having a ball.' Mostly she was lonely.

'Gran, what did you think when Pat was born?'

'I didn't think anything.'

'You didn't think about giving him away?'

'Who to?'

'You know. Nuns or something.'

Gran laughed. She held her crocheting, hook and square, and with her other practised hand lit a cigarette.

'But Grand-dad didn't feel the same. He didn't want Pat, did he?'

'Ask your grand-dad.'

'I asked Grand-dad. He wouldn't talk.' She hadn't known about Pat until she was twelve. 'You were up for Christmas, remember? You said Pat was in extended care or something. I asked who Pat was and Mom turned blue. Why the big secret?'

'Ask your mom.'

That winter Tina had got her first period. The fierce, turbulent emotions of the time, together with the sudden revelation of her uncle Pat, had caused her to turn a moral spotlight on her family. Exposed! Her mother was a sister with a half-numb heart, her grand-dad a deserting father. Only Gran had been able to stand the glare of Tina's scrutiny. Her brusqueness dissolved and even after the spotlight's beam was extinguished, her beautiful motives glowed.

'I wouldn't do it either, Gran.'

'Do what?'

'Give away my baby.'

'Jesus! You're not pregnant?'

In November Tina woke to the infamous grey sky, the curse of the wet feet. She slogged around soaked to the knees, shivering and wiping her nose on her sleeve. More than ever she felt like a hick, but now at least her loneliness corresponded only to the school timetable. When she came into Gran's kitchen and found Pat bibbed and curled fetal over his arms, she read his posture like this: The Thinker. 'Hello, Pat! Hello in there!' and it was like setting a metronome swinging. He'd rock with rising excitement until she took his slippery hand and pulled him to his toes. For Tina he bounced. For her he sang his moaning song. Quite without the expected effort, she returned his affection.

That right hand, the one always in his mouth, was the cleanest thing she'd ever seen. So pink and swollen the cruel hook of his lifeline was rendered harmless, his untrimmed nails soft. She dreamt of bringing Pat to school, leading him through the long corridors, his right hand high and not just clean, but radiant, a torch. This new light falling over them, the other students would see how shallow and cliquey they were. At the same time they'd recognize the opposite traits in Tina and be sorry for ignoring or smirking at her. Applause and tearful apology, the hallways would ring with it, like the clang clang clang of a cymbal and all the vibrations.

Then came Christmas. Gran said she wouldn't be going up north with Tina. 'I haven't made arrangements for Pat.'

'Bring Pat! Why not?'

'Pat disturbs people.'

'You mean Grand-dad? He's gone to Florida.'

'Home is where Pat's heart is. You know that.'

No one had wanted to institutionalize Pat – certainly not Francine, Gran's younger child, not even her husband Norm. Yet it had given Gran some relief to accuse them of it, especially in the early years before Pat could walk, when the strain pounded her thin. She was house-bound with a child who lay on a towel on the living-room floor nursing on his own hand because once he had swallowed and almost choked to death on his pacifier. Unable to sit, he couldn't even be taken out in a stroller. When Francine tore in after school, slamming doors, calling out her news of the day, Gran, from hours of silence and immobility, couldn't help but shout, 'What are you screaming for? Do you want to give Pat and me a heart attack? Do you want to see your brother in an institution?' Back then Francine used to take up the corners of Pat's towel and pull him through the house, 'Round, round the mulberry bush...' Gran always startled by the way Pat kicked his feet, joyfully, when all day he'd been lying motionless.

Then they learned where to have Pat diagnosed. At the

clinic they told Gran and Norm that Pat should've been walk-
ing years before. Gran should've treated Pat as she'd treated
Francine and his physical development would've been more
normal. Gran protested. 'How could I treat him the same as
Francine when all he does is lie on the floor like an old shoe?'
They replied, 'You limited him by your limited expectations.'

'Well, shit,' Gran told Norm as they drove home. 'I
should've been telling him all along he was gonna be an astronaut. Hey, Pat! You're gonna be an astronaut!' He was lying
face-down in the back saturating the seat with his drool.

After a year of therapy he could sit and hold objects. Later
he was able to walk after a fashion. But the most promising
change for Gran was when they discovered Pat's virtual blind-
ness and prescribed a pair of glasses. For the first time since his
birth nine years before, Gran made eye contact with her son.
His lids were red and lashless, eyes baubled by the
magnification of the lenses, but when she looked down into
the black entrance of his eye, he began to rock back and forth
and moan with unmistakable pleasure. Then she recognized
who Pat really was – the humble bearer of a love uncondi-
tional and unchanging. True, she hadn't expected anything of
him. Those years he lay on the living room floor, she hadn't
talked to or played with him, but sat on the couch smoking
and staring with bewildered revulsion. She'd had no idea what
was waiting for her.

Yet she continued to do well with the imaginary institution. When friends remarked on the miracle therapy had
worked on Pat, she cut in asking if she shouldn't commit him
and see if they could make him prime minister. Then Norm
got a job offer up north to manage a service station. It was back
in his home town and better work than he'd ever had in Vancouver.

'There isn't anything up there to help Pat,' Gran said.
'Should we go anyway and put him in an institution?'

'Is that what you want?' Norm asked.

'That's what *you* want.'

'I didn't say – '

'Exactly! You didn't say NO!'

She could always catch Norm in that trap, the one he would forever lay for himself, 'Is that what *you* want?' He wasn't very smart. She'd married him at seventeen, when he was on leave from the army.

Two years later the same offer, but this time she didn't trick him. He wanted Francine, then fourteen and listening to Elvis all weekend long behind her closed bedroom door.

For several years she and Pat drove up to visit Francine on school holidays. With Norm there too, they were almost a regular family. Then Francine graduated from high school and Gran saw Norm had allowed her to wear lipstick and hang off the arm of a boy. She'd forgotten about that kind of love. She hadn't slept with Norm since Francine was born; all those years with Pat had taught her something better. So if Francine was going to forget the lesson of her brother and run around like a floozy, Gran would consider her maternal responsibilities complete. Later, when she hardly ever saw Francine, Gran likened herself to a mother cat not acknowledging her own grown kitten. And if she ever felt the pang or twist of regret, or dwelt on what she had forfeited, she reminded herself that, unlike those two you-know-whos, at least she didn't bear the worse burden of guilt for having abandoned a retarded child.

Though Tina's Christmas absence called back all the pain of Francine's departure years before, Gran felt uncharacteristically positive. She chuckled, thinking of Tina hunched doggedly over her yarn, her afghan knotted and misshapen, looking more like a net to catch a whale. For Tina's work at bingo and telephone soliciting, she praised her endlessly to friends. Alone with her son: 'Weren't so many dishes in the sink when Tina was here, were there, Pat? Things are quiet around here without her. Right, Pat?'

When the telephone rang on New Year's Day, Gran could hear Tina snuffle even before she said hello.

'Oh, Gran! I can't come back! I've thought about it all through the holidays. It's that school. It's too awful.'

'Suit yourself,' Gran said. Then, 'Just a minute. I'm gonna put Pat on the phone. He wants to say goodbye.'

The receiver knocked against Pat's glasses. In the background, Gran: 'Grunt or something, Pat. Let Tina know you love her.'

Without a doubt she came back for her uncle Pat. 'He can't speak for himself, so we've got to be his voice, right?' She said this getting off the all-night bus, radiant with a selfless idealism that made Gran bite into her cigarette.

'There he is then, but don't get too close. He caught impetigo from some germ-bag at the Sunshine Christmas Club. Didn't you, Pat?'

Late in February, auditions. 'I'm in the lighting booth!' Tina said, beaming. Then she explained that rehearsals would keep her from Bingo. 'But I'll still flog those lightbulbs, Gran. I want to do my bit for Pat.'

The boy was wearing an old oversized trench coat, but his hair was neat, his lashes thick and long like some part of a tropical flower. Grinning, he stuck out his hand. 'I'm Pat.'

Gran was visibly taken aback. 'Come and meet the other Pat,' said Tina. They went into the kitchen, the boy's big coat flapping around his ankles. Pat was sitting on his child's seat in the corner, rocking.

'Ho! He looks like Woody Allen ... freeze-dried.'

Tina shrieked with laughter. At the sound of her voice, Pat's rocking accelerated. 'Look at this.' She got on her knees and pried Pat's hand from his mouth. 'His hands are so different! This one's softer and cleaner – '

'So?' said Gran.

Ten minutes later the young people had Pat bundled up and out in the yard, tossing a beach ball back and forth. Now and then the boy would get the ball to Tina by bouncing it off Pat's head, Pat springing on cue, sometimes toppling onto the wet lawn so Tina had to dash over and right him again. Pink ball, grey sky, Tina's new purple coat. Gran, watching from the window, dropped cigarette ash on the sill.

Later she prepared a hot bath for Pat. They'd brought him in soaked to his long underwear. Tina, on the other side of the closed bathroom door, asked, 'Isn't he nice, Gran?'

'Who?' Gran called back, taking Pat's arm out of his shirt.
'Pat!'
'Which Pat?'
'Ha ha. Very funny, Gran. My Pat!'
Gran didn't know she was so funny.
'Can I invite him for supper next week?'
Looking into the bathtub, she saw dozens of Tina's long permed hairs floating on the rising water. It made her gag. She scooped them out with the toilet brush and left it beside the sink for Tina to see.

'Did I tell you, Gran, Pat's a vegetarian?'
Too late. The boy was already standing there in the kitchen. He'd removed the trench-coat and was wearing a tweed blazer four sizes too large. 'Sorry, son,' said Gran. 'In this house we like the taste of blood.' He bent over laughing. They sat down and he served himself a mountain of mashed potatoes, making a hole in the centre of the mound and filling it with margarine. 'A butter volcano,' he told Gran.
All through the meal Gran found herself more and more appalled by their maturity. They were so mutually attentive and respectful, twining their feet together under the table, the boy listening to Tina with a wide open face.
'Are you coming to our final play, Gran?'
'*The Glass Menagerie*,' said Pat.
'What's your part, Pat?'
'He's not acting,' said Tina.
'I'm in the lighting booth.'
Gran winced and stubbed out her cigarette. It grated on her nerves the way they conversed in couplets. 'What do you two do in the lighting booth?'
They reddened, grinning like conspirators. 'We enhance the dramatic tension,' said Pat.
'We are the full moon, the stars, the rising and setting of the sun,' said Tina, hand on her heart.
'Not getting very far in your stage career, are you Tina?'
'I don't want to be an actress any more. I'm going into Special Education.'

'Twit!' Gran slammed her cup on the table, sloshing coffee. 'Why would you do a stupid thing like that? Why don't you do something you'll get a little thanks for?'

Tina felt sick the rest of the evening. She was ashamed of herself because she'd been embarrassed by Gran – the lit cigarette in the ashtray beside Gran's plate, the line of smoke that snuck across the table all through dinner. When Gran licked the rim of the salad dressing bottle before passing it to Pat, Tina thought she was going to die. Then, in the bathroom, she saw Gran had left the toilet brush on the vanity again and flecks of cigarette ash in cryptic patterns in the sink. Pat must have seen that, too.

All Tina wanted was for Gran and Pat to like each other. Gran was the person she loved and admired most, but she worried that Pat might not be able to see through Gran's smokescreen. Then, when she walked him to the bus stop, he told her, 'Your grandmother's the perfect dowdy divorcee. I love her.' Tina assailed him with relieved kisses. His father was a surgeon and his mother the editor of a women's magazine.

'Pat wants my afghan,' she told Gran later as they both sat crocheting in front of the TV. 'He says it's the greatest kitschiest afghan he's ever seen.' Gran said if Tina wasn't going to donate it to the MHS store, she ought to pay for the yarn.

'Sure. Sure I will. Are you mad at me, Gran?'

'Why should I be? Are you guilty of something?'

Tina blushed. She *was* guilty. In Pat's trench coat there was a pocket for everything. A pocket for a Walkman, for a notebook, hair gel, a hackey-sack. One pocket for safes. She was thinking about saying yes.

For months the rain's faint drumming had lulled and kept Tina in sleep. That night it no longer played on the metal awning over the front porch. But she'd been woken by a noise, maybe her uncle Pat, though it was unlike him – a low, rumbling groan, the staving off of pain or fear. By the time she'd groped her way out of bed and into the hallway, she'd changed her mind: a sexual sound. She came forward, curious and appalled. At the end of the hall, an outline of light behind the bathroom door, water running.

Pat's door was open a hand-space, pale gold slanting into the hall. She nudged the door and it swung open to show him sitting on the edge of his bed, naked. The light in the room came from a Christmas bulb in the Dumbo lamp on his bed-side table. It cast him in a yellow glow, his back with its con-stellation of moles facing her, head bowed, tiny loose buttocks squashed down on the plastic sheet. Why was the bed stripped? She was going to call, oh Pat, when she saw his shadow on the wall, distorted, elongated, stretching him out to the size of a normal man.

The bathroom door crashed open, flooding the hall with light. 'Jesus! Do you want to give me a heart attack?' The front of Gran's nightie, made sheer by wetness, clung to her. Through the nylon fabric, a dark nipple the size of a saucer.

'What?' Gran snapped. 'He shit everywhere. Go back to bed.'

It wasn't just the tone of her grandmother's voice but the whole situation brought to light. The kind of life Gran really had. Pat's silhouette. Suddenly Tina was sobbing. She turned and ran back to her room.

Gran had heard the same sound as Tina, had risen to find Pat rolling around in his own diarrhea. She'd sponged him down and, in the tub, soaked and rinsed the bedsheets, then gone back to bed and endured an hour of Tina's unmusical blubbering. Finally, she hovered over sleep again.

Something outside her window shrieked.

Gran heaved herself out of bed and peered through the slit in the curtain. In the warm circle of the porch lamp, an orange cat was slowly unfolding herself, reclining indulgently, licking her shoulder. Such coy gestures, Gran knew she couldn't be alone. Back in the shadows, she spotted the square-headed singer humped down low. The moment he resumed his rum-bling serenade, Gran understood. This was the secret animal life. This was wooing. She couldn't even imagine how Norm had wooed her that first time. All she remembered was she'd enjoyed it and become pregnant with Pat. The way the tom was yowling now seemed like fear. She'd been afraid then, too.

Norm's fish-mouth opening and closing as he thrashed on top of her. A hundred surprising spasms. So long ago.

Gran drew the curtain aside. The reclining cat reared. For minutes she crouched in the spotlight, estral eyes fixed on Gran. Then she began a slow hypnotic slink to the window. Hair rose on Gran's neck. She felt stalked, not by the cat, but an instinct. Felt it dangerously close and coming closer. Gasping, she broke away. All night she shivered in bed, ear open to plangent impulse. Water dripped off the awning – a sound like smacking lips.

The next evening Pat and Tina clumped down the basement stairs to the rumpus room. Their laughter carried, not their words. Gran got up and turned off the television, stood for a moment listening.

The heat register in the dining room was just above the rumpus room sofa. She would have to crawl under the dining room table. Flipping aside the plastic tablecloth, she dropped to her knees, lay on her belly, feet in their crocheted slippers jutting out from under the table. With her ear pressed into the metal grating of the register, she could hear them clearly, necking for sure, a sound like they were sharing some watery piece of fruit. And the boy moaning softly, Tina mumbling some mild kind of protest.

She stayed. Stayed for the full story of her granddaughter's love-making: all the modulations of their breathing and laughter, that old couch knocking a happy code against the basement wall, their grunting climax. Then, as they were quietly recovering, Gran crawled out from under the table. Smiling grimly, she went to the telephone.

'You better wire some money down here. Tina's going home.'

The familiar silence of the girl Francine stopped dead by a word like 'institution'. 'Is she in trouble?'

'You know.'

'No, I don't...'

'Sex,' said Gran. 'In my basement.'

'Oh, God!' cried Francine. 'Give her a break! You know how

lonely she was. Is he a decent boy? Is she taking precautions?'

'I want her out of here!'

'Dog in the manger, that's what you are! A dog in the manger!'

And while Gran was still arguing on the phone, Tina and Pat crept up the stairs hand in hand, Tina's face all rosy, her hair wet around her forehead. She gestured that they were going out, wiggled her fingers and blew Gran a kiss.

Francine wouldn't listen, so Gran finally hung up. With the young people gone, she felt strangely at a loss. She went into Pat's room and stood at the end of his bed. For a long time she watched him sucking on his fist in his sleep. Dreaming. He must be dreaming. That other Pat, the boy who was just now downstairs catching his breath, his love will go. Go like the fine wash of ecstasy that flowed over him. This gave her some comfort. She fished in her pocket for another cigarette.

THE HANGING GARDENS OF BABYLON

'OKAY YOU TWO, go on out now and play,' said their father. But because the room was dim, an old dark blanket slung over the curtain rod, he was half hidden in the corner and they had forgotten him. They did not listen now.

There was an unpleasant smell in the room, sour and oppressive; it came from their mother. She lay motionless on the bed, small like a child, her white face passive with discomfort. At her mother's feet Lillian sat watching her brother Rudy, thinking that he didn't know anything. Half on, half off the bed, he was clutching their mother's hand and chatting happily. 'Here's a little man, Mommy, going for a walk,' he said, smiling. With his two fingers he began to march up her arm, 'Dee dee dee, dee dee dee,' soft temporary impressions in the white flesh. He crossed her shoulder, turned, and his walking fingers moved gently over her breast. At the base of her stomach, rising under the quilt like a jelly mould, he stopped and in his play-voice squealed, 'My, what a big hill!'

'Rudy!' Their father's voice was sharp and tired. 'That's enough. Lillian, take him and go get the mail. You can see Mommy again later.'

She got up mechanically and tugged Rudy by the arm. 'I don't wanna go!' but Lillian easily removed him, forced his small thrashing form through the door, then slipped out herself, looking back for just an instant to see their mother, white-faced, cover her eyes with her hand.

Quietly, sock-footed, Lillian descended the stairs to the kitchen, Rudy trailing. A week ago their mother had taken to bed and it showed, especially in that room. The table was cluttered with cereal boxes and Rudy's toys. Puss-Love's paw prints marked the counters like a pattern in the Arborite. No one had remembered to feed Puss-Love. They themselves had been eating out of cans and boxes. Last night was Easter, the very death and rebirth of their Lord, and in celebration they had had Kraft Dinner and no chocolate eggs. This had made them both cry, Rudy at the table, *Jesus wants for me to have an egg!* and Lillian later, when she was alone. The garbage overflowed in the corner and, curiously, a pair of Rudy's underpants lay on the floor next to the refrigerator. Lillian looked in the bread box. She said, talking into the box, her voice sounding hollow, 'There's just crusts. You want one?'

'Yes,' said Rudy. 'Yes, please.'

Earlier Lillian had put the peanut butter in the cookbook drawer so she would not have to keep dragging a chair over to reach the cupboard. But there was no clean cutlery. She eyed the sink full of cold greasy water and most of their everyday dishes. 'Go to the china cabinet and get a knife.'

'I'm not allowed,' said Rudy.

'Go on.'

Frowning, he left the kitchen, then came back with a letter-opener. Lillian used it anyway. They put on coats and rubber boots and, taking the mail key from the hook behind the door, went out with their crusts.

'I wanna carry the key,' said Rudy.

'You'll lose it.'

'You always say that.'

'Because I know you will.'

They sat on the front steps watching Poke run around on the wet brown lawn. Every few minutes Rudy called out, 'Poke! Here, Poke! Poke! Poke! Poke!' spraying sandwich, the dog ignoring him, not even barking, just circling foolishly in his matted sheepdog coat.

'Wanna get a stick and play with Poke?' he asked.

'We have to get the mail.'

'What do you wanna do after that?'

'I don't know,' said Lillian, dropping the remainder of her crust and standing. She went down the steps and walked the length of the driveway, shuffling and kicking the gravel.

'Hey, wait!' Rudy called, leaping down and racing after her. 'Wait for me!'

The way to the mailbox was an old asphalt road patched

everywhere with wavering lines of tar. On both sides a dirty crust of melting snow filled the ditches. Aspen scrub, strung with last year's wind-sent debris, screened the black and saturated fields. Pervasive the odour of wet soil, the bright biting green smell of new leaves. Rudy went with his face up and nostrils wide, she behind, hands deep in pockets. They heard the call of one bird to another, dee dee dee, dee dee dee, the answer in variation meaning yes, no, perhaps – meaning, *yes, soon.*

They had walked for several minutes when Rudy slowed and began to talk to himself. He mumbled first, then half-sang, making shapes in the air with his fingers, watching rapt as if it were not he who made them, as if the shapes were independent living creatures. They were contortions of his hands, claw-like animals that flew short distances, tethered to the ends of his arms.

'Hurry up.'

But he did not hear her. He growled, laughed, said 'No! No!' then stopped in his tracks. He pointed and shouted, voice shrill with excitement. 'Lookit! Lookit, Lilly!'

A dead cat in the middle of the road. They approached and, standing over it, stared. Rudy made the sign of the cross.

'Whose cat do you think it is?' he asked solemnly.

It had been run over several times. The head was intact, but the body almost completely flattened. It lay gape-mouthed on a star-shaped stain of its own making. Rudy squatted and peered in the mouth. 'There's bugs or something living in here. Look, Lillian.'

'I don't want to,' she said, but kneeled and looked anyway.

Small white worms, like grains of rice, tumbled out of the throat. On the wide crusted-over eye was a pivoting fly. They remained there, in the middle of the road, crouching silently.

'You know what Daddy told me?' Lillian said. 'He said that tomorrow they're going to take Mommy and cut her stomach open to get the baby. Cut her open to pull the baby out. What do you think will happen when they do that?'

Rudy did not reply.

'What do you think happens to people when they get cut open like that?'

Rudy still looked at the cat.

'Answer me.'

'Poor cat,' said Rudy, patting its head gently.

She opened her mouth to tell him again but there came a sudden screaming blare, a car bearing down on them, horn pressed. They froze, still hunkering, not even resigned, not anything. The car swerved. Just beyond, it came to an angry halt. The driver opened the door and, leaning out, shouted at them. 'Stupid kids! What the hell are you doing in the middle of the road!'

Lillian hauled Rudy to his feet and dragged him along without looking back at the car, her heart slamming around inside her. Rudy was silent and trembling. A few yards on something dawned on him.

'Lilly! We almost had an accident! We almost had an accident!'

Skipping ahead, swinging his arms like berserk pendulums, leaping, he sang for joy. 'Accident! Accident!'

'Did you hear what I told you!'

Rudy turned and smiled. 'It's not true.'

'It *is* true!'

He faced her fully, taking on the pose of a pugilist, fists clenched and threatening, jaw jutting.

'Oh, cut it out, you,' she said, and he deflated.

They walked on.

Rudy came back beside her. He tugged on her sleeve until she withdrew her hand and held his. 'Lilly! Tell me about those wonderful things.'

'What wonderful things?'

'The seven wonderful things.'

'Oh. You mean the seven wonders of the world. I told you yesterday. I told you a hundred times.'

'Tell me again.'

She sighed. She had read it all in a book, weeks ago. 'The statue of Memnon cries for his mother.'

'He's a baby. What about the other statue?'

'The Colossus? That's a huge one, I don't remember where.

He stands over the water like this.' She straddled her legs. 'The sea goes under him.'

Rudy laughed. 'He's peeing in the water.'

She pursed her lips and let go of his hand. Rudy reddened. 'Sorry,' he said ruefully. 'Sorry.' She took him back, putting both their hands in her pocket.

'And what about the gardens! Those gardens you told me about!'

'The hanging gardens of Babylon.'

'Yes!' he shouted. 'Go. Talk about them.'

She did and smiled a little for she knew a lot and liked to say what she knew. She told him about the five rising terraces, two hundred and fifty feet high.

Rudy looked straight up at the sky.

The spiral staircase, the queen's look-out, the animals.

'What kind of animals?'

'Cats, dogs, snakes.'

'Pigs?'

'Yes, pigs,' she said.

'What else?'

'All animals.'

'*Which ones?* Tell me,' he said, cross.

'Elephants, hawks, chickens, lady bugs, hyenas...' She continued until, satisfied, he asked, 'Which plants?'

'All plants. That's all I'll say.'

'Lilies?' he asked, smiling and squeezing her hand.

'I said all plants.'

'Easter lilies,' he said.

They were in sight of the mailbox. They had passed a few acreages belonging to neighbour families and now the tree stands were denser and the snow was gone from the ditches, bright green shoots rising on either side like the tips of soft, coloured bayonets. The air was fetid, mildew in the grass, last season's dead newly thawed. Rudy beamed. 'I think those gardens are so nice. Where are they?'

'In Babylon.'

'Where's Babylon?'

'Far far away. In a desert.'

'I'd like to live there. I'd like to live there with you. Let's pretend we're there now.'

'You pretend,' said Lillian. 'I'll watch you.'

Rudy began to creep along the road, making exaggerated sweeping gestures with his arms as if he were pushing back foliage. Every few steps he stopped and shaded his eyes with his hands saying, 'Hullo, who's hanging in the garden of boobilon?' Then they were at the mailbox and a boy in a plaid jacket and a toque that read PUT ON A HAPPY FACE stood there staring at Rudy and Lillian.

'Give me the key,' Rudy said.

'You're too little.' She opened the compartment.

'Ours was empty too,' said the boy with the toque. 'It's a holiday, remember?' He was staying at his grandparents' for Easter, he told them. His face was dirty, some orange sauce circling his mouth. He tilted back his head and narrowed his eyes. 'I got a secret.'

'What kind of secret?' asked Rudy.

'Come on,' he said.

They followed him back in the direction they had just come from, the boy looking for something in the ditch. 'This is it,' he said finally.

Together they jumped the ditch and pushed through the aspen scrub into the trees. Then they found themselves standing in a small clearing beside a shallow pond formed by spring run-off. All around and rising up through the trees like cathedral music was the deep, frantic, pulsing sound of frogs. It was hurried and overlapping, repetitive, an urgent chorus like mass in amphibian tongue. A plastic bucket sat next to the pond. The boy went over to it and beckoned.

They came and looked inside. The bucket was half-full of water and teeming with frogs, coupled frogs, one in front that made the motions of swimming, one in back with its ridiculous arms clutching the other's middle. This seemed like such an absurd thing for a frog to be doing, squeezing the breath out of another, not letting go even when the boy put his hand in and stirred.

'Isn't that funny?' said Rudy.

Lillian glanced at the boy and at Rudy who swayed as if the sound had hands to move him, then back at the frogs. 'What are they doing?' she asked.

'Fucking,' said the boy.

He waded into the pond and, splashing around, caught up a handful of doubled frogs. Returning to the bucket, he dropped them in.

'What are they doing?' asked Lillian.

'I told you. They're fucking. You know what fucking is, don't you?'

'Of course,' said Lillian.

'Isn't it funny?' said Rudy.

She looked again in the bucket at the piggy-back frogs swimming in circles, cycling around and around, no beginning or end. The frog song seemed louder now, insistent, listen-listen-listen. She was dizzy, then afraid, of the song and the strange boy, this hidden centrifugal clearing revolving with frogs. Clearing, earth, everything, turning, circling.

The boy took Rudy's hand and guided it into the bucket. Rudy drew back quickly and laughed. Listen-listen-listen. The song lulled and agitated. She put her hands on her ears. The way the boy held a pair of frogs, learning their weight, they were something to throw. Listen-listen-listen.

'Funny!' cried Rudy.

'What are you going to do?' she asked.

He shrugged, then wound back his arm. Even airborne the frogs did not uncouple. They sailed straight for a tree, struck it – a terrible jellied splash on the bark.

They ran some of the way, then Rudy was tired and Lillian had to carry him on her back. He was no extra strain for her now, after the things she knew and had seen. She walked thinking of the swerving car, the bulging cat eye, her mother's skin, the bright gelatin stain on the tree. Rudy had his legs twined around her middle and was singing, 'Dee dee dee, dee dee dee...' When she came to the dead cat, she passed it hurriedly.

'Let me down now,' he said. 'Please.'

She walked slowly so Rudy would not fall behind, but still

he dragged along at the end of her arm, yawning. He was rubbing his fist in his eye.

'How much more till we're home?'

'Just a bit.'

Then a moment later he announced, 'I know what was happening to those frogs.'

'Which frogs?' She meant the frogs in the pail or the frogs on the tree.

'All the frogs.'

'You don't.'

'I do! You think I don't know anything but I know lots! And I know what was happening to those frogs!'

'What then?'

'They were going to the hanging gardens.'

And suddenly she was furious. 'Don't you know there's no hanging gardens of Babylon? Have you ever heard of that place before? There's no such place as Babylon! It's *made up!*'

She was shaking and he was backing away from her with a fierce angry face.

'There is so!' he cried. 'Too bad, Lilly. Too bad you don't know where Babylon is.'

'There is no Babylon!'

Rudy ran away up the road.

Through the aspen stand the breeze was filtering. Again she heard that call, dee dee dee, dee dee dee – the bird-call, Rudy-call, then the sound of snow melting in the ditch. Gradually the sound grew louder, becoming the roar of a river, of a waterfall, water gushing up out of the open earth, pushing things forward. She saw the tumble of waking insects on the crest, and animals, cats, dogs, snakes, all animals, *which ones? tell me*, all animals and people, sweeping forward, on and on and on to the beginning again. Listen-listen-listen. Listen-listen-listen.

When Rudy finally disappeared, a dark bird flew by. She watched as it dipped and swooped and circled, circled again. Then it vanished too, in the direction of Babylon. Everything in the direction of Babylon.

OIL AND DREAD

A JOLT. Wide-open eyes. Every day now Des wakes like this, disoriented, a man who has been moved in his sleep. A whisper, his mother's name for him, disturbs like a finger traced around his ear. Finally, Ita's rolling over in the bed delivers him, brings time and place. Her waxy face surfaces and inhales. She is swimming in sleep. Des slides out of bed and picks from the clothes horse his big trousers, a shirt the size of a sail. He dresses as he moves through the small rooms, leaving the house before both arms are in his jacket.

In this treeless place the wind reveals itself in the unceasing transport of clouds, the swelling of crows on the power lines to larger, more ragged forms. Reeled in again to the water, he follows a dry-stone wall that disappears where its parts have been returned to the ground. Past Feely's, Ita's store, the dirty windows and milk boxes and lottery tickets that make them their living. Near the beach stands an abandoned cottage. Its rotten thatch, shiny like threads of mica, sags and stops the door. Des wades thigh-deep through nettles, leans in the paneless window. Inside, all is as it was left when years ago the vanished occupant made his break with Ireland. The blankets, drawn back on the bed, are marbled now with mildew. On a table soft with dust, a tin mug from that last breakfast.

A stone falls from the wall behind him. Des starts, smashing his head on the sill, then stands rubbing the spot: where Ita claims God touched him with His Mighty Finger when Des became a Catholic to marry her and a perfect circle of bald appeared. He is bleeding.

The dog cowers by the fence, ears flat against its black head. Its eyes roll upward as in pictures of the martyred saints.

'Fuck you.'

Its tongue fawns. What Des cannot stand, even in his own

dog: anything like submissiveness. With his foot, he raises the muzzle up, up until he can grab it and feel the throat block with straining. When he lets go, the dog pauses on its haunches licking around its mouth. It blinks, then bounds away toward the water.

A flock of crows blows in like paper ash. The frustrated beat of the ocean. Weekends, he brings his daughters here, makes them say, as he points to the blurred false-front of Ireland's own distant coast, 'Mayo' and 'Sligo' and for a joke, 'Newfoundland'. Now this shore is home to his dread. Whatever threatens him, he feels for certain from here it will come, from the water – doom or a boat-load of judges.

The dog is barking. Its tail flails as it shuttles in the surf. Tug-of-war: dog and bird.

'Hey! Leave off!' Des crosses the beach to where they are battling. At his feet, the dog is jawing a live wing. The bird, black throat open in soundless rage, twists and thrashes and rocks the dog's obstinate head. It hisses at Des, panicked bravado. Des grins. With the side of his boot he kicks the dog away.

Des needs all the strength of his big hands to clutch the bird to his chest. 'I-i-i-ta!' He hammers the bed with his boot. Finally she sits up, blond hair sticking to the sides of her face as she groans at the ceiling. In Des's arms the bird convulses then, loosening a wing, flaps wildly, hisses. Ita gapes. 'What are you after bringing home now, you fucking – '

'Give me a hand.' He goes into the kitchen and from there can hear her fall out of bed and stumble around the room. 'You're an eejit, Desmond Martin. What time is it? Didn't you hear me up half the night with the Old Man and his pissing and moaning? Jesus! Some of us have a funeral to go to today! You and your creeping around at all godless hours. It's a sin.'

She appears in bare feet, her nightdress, a green housecoat. Cigarette between her lips, she heads to the gas range for a light.

'Ita!'

'What? Can't I have a fag?'

'Will you look what I've got in my arms!'

She faces the bird and softens. The cigarette goes in her pocket. 'What happened?'

'Oil.'

'Poor thing.' She begins taking the dirty dishes out of the sink. 'Des, you are a saint and a lover of the wee animals.'

When the sink is filled with soapy water, Des, so he can take off his jacket, has Ita hold the bird. It wrenches free immediately, smashing its wings against the counter, sloshing water on Ita and the floor. It stabs at Des's eye with the lance of its beak.

'Jesus, Ita!'

'Jesus, you!' she shrieks.

He wrestles with its beating wings. The bird collides with the window, jettisons a spray of liquid shit that just misses Ita. She screams: 'The devil's in it! Fuck off! Fuck off!' When at last he recaptures it, beak in his fist, wings in the vice of his huge hand, Ita is laughing. 'A hell of a way to get up in the morning!'

She takes a Brillo pad and begins scrubbing the bird. 'Was there oil on the beach?'

'None.'

Hers is not to question mystery. She changes the subject. 'You didn't hear the Old Man last night crying for his dead brother? Course not or you wouldn't have been up at the crack of day! I had to lay out all his gear in the middle of the night.' She pauses and sniffs. 'Do you think we should have brought the girls up?'

'A funeral's no place for kids.'

'At Mary's age I loved a funeral.' She squints at him. 'You'd be happy to leave our poor babes in Letterkenny all the year, wouldn't you? You don't love your daughters.'

He sees where she is leading him. Her regular accusation. The girls come home every weekend.

'You don't. Not like I do. Every day's misery without them. I mean it when I say I'd have ten more if you'd only get a job.'

She drains the soapy water, refills the sink. Next, Des knows, she will remind him he is Canadian.

Under her breath: 'Sure there's more work in Canada...'

The bird twists in his hands.

'This is the only thing I have to say: when the Old Man dies – God forgive me for mentioning such a thing on the very day we put his brother in the ground – when he dies we're all going to Canada.'

'We are not going to Canada!' Des roars.

'Why not? Sure you've never shown any kind of love for this country!'

He scoops the bird out of the sink, trailing a watery skirt. With its head suddenly free, it screeches, snakes a long neck toward Ita.

'Jesus!' She ducks.

Des leaves her standing in chaos. The dog has been waiting outside and is eager at his heel, but he shuts it out of the shed. He kicks clear an area on the dirt floor then shifts the spasming bird under his arm, stoops to lay down a bed of old newspapers.

Back in the house, Ita leans into the mop, dragging long on her cigarette. Her housecoat is drenched.

'What do you want?' Des asks from the door. 'Sausages? I'll run over to the store.'

She won't look at him. 'I want you out of this hairy mood.'

'What mood?'

'So tight-lipped and always sneaking down to the beach. It has to do with that Canadian boy you wouldn't bring home the other night, doesn't it?'

'Will you get off that?'

'Then it's your not drinking any more. It's the Total Abstinence Society of the Sacred Heart around here. Cutting yourself off altogether isn't healthy.' She glances at him, then doubles full-face. 'Did you take that off the clothes horse?'

He looks down at himself, shirt-front ruined with the molasses-stain of oil.

'Is that your pressed white shirt for the funeral?' She takes the mop in her hands, a weapon, and comes raging after him.

The Old Man is sitting on the edge of the bed cleaning his nose with his little finger. He seems to be looking across the room where the red Christmas bulb burns continuously under the picture of the Sacred Heart. Des coughs and the Old Man looks up, frowning. He wipes his finger on the front of his undershirt and crosses himself.

'We're putting the brother in the ground today,' he says. 'Pray for Peter Feely.'

'He was a good man.' As he says this it occurs to Des that he hasn't thought of his own brother in years.

'No, he wasn't. He was just too old to be bad.'

'I'm going to dress you. Have you washed?'

'I don't wash.'

'Don't tell Ita that.'

'*You* don't tell her.'

Des gets the Old Man's underwear from the bureau. Slowly, the Old Man raises his arms, thin, stained in patches the colour of tea. Des peels the undershirt off his trunk, over his head, then is startled to see he has left him completely naked.

'Jesus,' says the Old Man. He waves his wormy hands in the air. A fumbling with the fresh shirt, an attempt to guide shaking hands into arm holes, but the Old Man is tangled in his own underwear. To hide what shames him, he draws up the round bulbs of his knees. Finally, his flushed face appears, glaring indignantly, showing the raw gums behind his lip. Des offers his forearm. The Old Man clutches it without meeting his eye, hoists himself onto bare bowed legs.

'Did Ita hammer you on the head?'

'What?'

'There's blood where your poll is bare.'

Des bends and takes an ankle, pushes a horny foot through the leg-hole of the briefs. Scrotum long on the thigh, translucent and fine as waxed paper. The Old Man smells of tobacco and urine.

'Has there ever been an oil slick around here?' Des asks.

'When I was a lad, there was a fellow away in the head. He wouldn't take communion. Used to do business down by the beach, what I don't know. Knocking stones together. One day doesn't a big wave roll up and snatch him away? We all went down and waited for the body to be spat back up. And when it came... What d'you think?'

'I don't know.' Des straightens and tucks the undershirt into the briefs, lowers the Old Man back onto the bed.

'Guess.'

'I don't know.'

'Well, what are we talking about, man!'

'I don't know what *you're* talking about.'

'Oil! He was blackened all over with oil. Black like his very own soul!'

'You're full of it,' says Des.

They struggle into the shirt, Des's great fingers grappling with the small buttons. Then he crosses the room and lifts the kilt that Ita has left spread over the back of a chair.

'Bonnet on his chest, Peter Feely will be buried in the costume of the Blue Raven Pipe Band.'

He gives the Old Man his arm again so he can stand and step into the kilt. A grey-and-blue plaid, it makes the Old Man look thin and white as a stick of chalk. 'You look great yourself.'

The Old Man sniffs loudly. 'I suppose Ita thinks that since I'll be decked out same as the corpse, I'll follow quick to the grave.'

'She doesn't.'

'You can tell her I don't intend to die.'

Des laughs. With the diaper pins Ita left on the bureau, he fixes the kilt through the Old Man's shirt to his underwear.

'Then again, oh Jesus, if I never die Ita'll get tired of waiting and go off to Canada anyway without me.'

'Listen. No one's going to Canada. All this bloody talk about Canada.'

'It'd be a terrible thing to be left behind, a whole ocean of water between us. Who in the world'd fix my tea?'

Almost a month ago Des met that boy in the pub. Ita introduced him to Des as his 'wee countryman'. Afterward, neither could recall his name. They knew his face though: fresh and amazed. Later Ita would describe the dimple in his chin as the place where God's Mighty Finger had touched him when he was in the womb.

He was touring Europe on his break from university. 'At last I hit Ireland, an English-speaking country. I head straight for the pub where I can get some conversation. This old guy accosts me. Yaks for hours. Finally, I tell him I can't understand a word he's saying. He's totally surprised. *You're* very clear, he says!'

'It's not the accent that gets me,' said Des. 'It's how bloody long it takes them to get to the point!'

The boy leaned forward and looked at Des earnestly. 'Talk to me, man. I love the boring, flat sound of your voice.'

When Ita left with a pint for the Old Man waiting at home, they were all drunk. She whispered in Des's ear: 'Bring that poor little fucking Canadian home. He can sleep on the sofa.'

'Whisky?' Des asked. He went to the bar and bought a bottle. 'Sorry it's not CC.'

'S'okay,' said the boy. 'I can get that any time.'

The publican roared for everyone to clear out, but they were only half finished the bottle. Outside the moon shone on the backs of the men talking in the yard. Des cradled the whisky in one arm, took the boy on the other and led him around the pub to where the mountain's silhouette was a crouching animal. A rutted road ran straight up the slope, a track for driving sheep and the turf-cutters' donkey carts.

They had climbed for a few minutes when Des started to laugh. 'Ita says bring that poor little fucking Canadian home.' Then he sang it: 'Brr-ing that poooor little fuck-ing Can-ay-dian hooome!'

'Ita's great,' said the boy. 'Ita's wild.'

'First time I slept with Ita....' From both sides of the track the panicked drumming of fleeing sheep. 'She got ... she brought out her account book from the store. Wrote: I solemnly swear... I will marry Ita Mary Feely!'

'And you had to sign!'

'That's not all! Had to swear and sign on the line I'd convert!'

The boy whistled. 'She's tough all right.'

'In here, man.' They had come to a half-ruined shed, three stone walls, a roof of corrugated iron. They fell inside, righting themselves to a view from high above the houses, pub, Ita's store. Des unscrewed the cap and drank, passed the whisky to the boy who could barely find his own mouth with the bottle.

'How 'bout them Blue Jays?' said Des.

They began to snicker again, Des first, the boy catching it. They were both buckled over and howling before Des could put in words the rest of his story. Finally: 'I had a laugh on Ita.' Heart pumping wildly, leaning into the boy, he slurred. 'Ita's account book? Didn't write my name. Wrote a different name so she wouldn't have anything on me. Desmond Martin. She was howling mad, not because she knew it wasn't my name, but because she'd been calling me Martin all along, see? I said everybody called me Martin, but she wouldn't have any such fucking coarseness, people calling each other by their surnames.'

'What's your name then?'

'Martin Sinclair! Desmond was the name of my dog.'

Now they were in agony, hysteria. Des could not breathe. He pounded his foot on the earth floor, whisky overturning, both scrambling to save it, then lying in silence, aching. Eventually, Des dragged himself out to urinate. The boy called after him, 'Lucky your dog wasn't named Spot!'

'Still ... there's more!' Des staggered up the slope so he could urinate on the metal roof of the shed. 'Already married, kid on the way – ' Then his voice drowned in the rush of liquid drumming.

When he crawled back into the shed, the boy hooted. 'How'd you get out of it?'

'Didn't. Ita doesn't know. Church don't know. Priest was a fossil. I think he died the day after. He'd married Ita's old man, too, for Christ's sake!'

'Jesus. There's a word for that...'

'Lots of words. Fucking-against-the-law are some of them.' He could see the boy's amazement. To Des it was clear what the joke had turned into: this was how much he had come to love Ita.

'She was pregnant?'

'Not Ita! Back in T.O. *Shit ... Did I say that!*' Des laughed and felt around for the bottle. 'It's fourteen years dead. I was your age, for Christ's sake. I never told anyone before.'

Silence. Des wondered if the boy had passed out. He took another swig of whisky, the after-taste suddenly caustic.

'Asshole,' said the boy.

Des shoved him hard against the wall, then, laughing, let him go. The boy struggled to his feet, lurched forward and out of the shed, groaning. Des poured over his own head the remaining whisky. Cold down the contours of his face, it seeped in and burned his eyes.

He thought the boy had gone out to urinate. 'Oh, Canada!' A minute later: 'Fucking little Can-ay-dian!' Now Des stumbled out of the hiding place, into the wide open side of the mountain, white light, cold face of the moon. The boy was gone.

Ita sets the teapot in the middle of the table. The Old Man, still in his piper's costume, bonnet askew, sucks on his gums and stares straight ahead. After a long silence, he sniffs. 'Aye, we buried him well.'

With a long even-toned cry, Ita collapses onto the table. Her back begins to tremble and her hands open wide like fans. Soon she is shaking the table, sobbing, the teapot lid rattling.

The Old Man sneers. 'Shut up, Ita. It's too late for the banshee.'

She straightens, face red, smeared with tears and mascara. She forces out her jaw and her fist hammers the table with such force that the Old Man quivers. 'Fuck you!' Ita roars. 'Who was up all night listening to your pissing and moaning? I was, you bastard!' Back of her hand over her forehead, she rolls her eyes, imitating the Old Man. 'Me God, me brother's dead and I'm the last of the true Blue Ravens! Me God, I never liked him and in heaven he'll know it, too! I'm afraid to die meself!'

The Old Man turns red and sniffs.

'Lay off him, Ita,' says Des.

'Don't you tell me what to do!' Suddenly she springs from

her chair and lunges for Des, grabs a handful of hair in one hand, smacks him again and again with the other.

'I-i-i-ta!' He sinks into her breasts, trying to push her away. The Old Man claps his hands, cackling. Then Ita falls forward with her arms around Des's neck, sobbing again, shuddering.

'Oh, Jesus!' she cries. 'Oh, Jesus! My uncle is dead and my children are in Letterkenny!'

Both men give up a roar of laughter. Ita, tears suspended, rises on her knees. 'That's funny?'

'Shhh.' Des pulls her close.

'With that eejit's carrying on, I didn't get my sleep. I'm exhausted. I don't know what I'm doing.'

'Ach,' says the Old Man. 'If you don't know, Ita, then we're surely lost.'

'What's the matter with you, Des? Why won't you tell me? Don't you love me any more?'

'More than ever.'

The Old Man mutters as they kiss. He clears his throat. Now that Ita is off her guard, he takes the opportunity to expectorate into his saucer.

'Des, something bad is going to happen. I feel it.'

The Old Man looks up, crossing himself alarmedly.

'Shhh.' Des kisses Ita again, then pours a cup of tea and puts it in her hands. She takes her chair. For a long time they sit in silence, then the Old Man begins a long recounting of the funeral events.

'I'll go and have a look at that bird,' says Des.

It is not where he left it on the newspaper. He finds it behind some paint cans, wings half-spread, head lowered. Reaching down, he wags his fingers, expecting assault. The bird does not move. It has stiffened in the corner trying to extend wide its wings where there is no space, trying to stretch out its life. The black eye is still a shiny bead. Des carries it out of the shed and throws it over the stone wall into his neighbour's field.

Ita is undressing in the bedroom. In a half-slip and brassiere, she is hanging her black dress in the wardrobe.

'The bird's dead.'

'Not another body to bury. I've had enough.'

'I'm going up the mountain to see if a slick's coming in.'

'You're away in the head! I thought you were going to open the shop!'

He is already in the car when she appears at the front door clutching closed her blouse and waving to him. He unrolls the window.

'Leave something at the holy well for my uncle!'

Earlier that afternoon he drove in the funeral cortege, the Old Man beside him, Ita in back leaning over the seat to brush her father's shoulders or straighten his baldric. The Old Man stared ahead at the pipers marching on either side of the hearse. Finally, he passed comment. 'That's a bloody noise they're making.' When Des turned around to look at Ita, he saw how the procession trailed, mourners in black fighting the wind.

Later at the grave site, Des was one of the men lowering the coffin into the earth. The rope did not burn or harm his hands. The coffin was as light as if they were burying Peter Feely's soul without his body. As they worked, hand-over-hand, the Old Man stood at the top of the grave with the big drum. Head high, dried bloom on the long neck of a plant gone to seed, jaw set, staring fiercely.

Coffin in place, they drew the ropes out of the grave and waited in silence, mourners' feet apart to brace against the wind, priest's robes swollen and rippling. They were watching the Old Man as he slowly raised the baton. He poised, a salute, mourners suspended. From a distance, the falling broken voice of a crow. When his arm finally dropped, the drum sounded relief – a hollow bottomless beat stronger than the wind's hoarse breathing. Then, as if in retaliation, the wind snatched the Old Man's bonnet from his head and set it sailing through the tombstones.

And the power of the Old Man's sacrifice for his dead brother, all his strength in a sound, rocked Des and gave him the vision of his own brother. He saw him at age thirteen or fourteen, bird-cage bare-chested, hair raised on his head and mouth torn open, a scream of indignation, some long-forgotten injustice. The first time Des had thought of his brother in years was earlier that day, dressing the Old Man. He was puzzled why he remembered him again, in childhood now instead of as he had seen him last, in his twenties, grown to manhood. Drum sounded again. The scream persisted. Peter Feely's daughter was keening for him.

Driving through the village, Des does a double-take. A boy on a bicycle waves at him and for a second Des thinks it is the Canadian. He sees one almost every day now, these look-alikes, pretend Canadians, and wonders where they have suddenly come from. Passing the pub, he continues up the mountain until he meets a herd of sheep chewing cud in the middle of the road. They do not start or move when he sounds the horn. Only when he opens the door and steps onto the road do they heave and bolt. Minutes later, the road runs out. He has driven most of the way up the mountain and will now follow on foot the ridge of its naked back.

The first part of the ascent is steep, a muddy sheep track around broken faces of stone. The heather, past its prime, is a cover of papery blossoms faded brown and coral. His big boot misses the track, sinks into the peat and sometimes scrapes away the green skin of the mountain, exposing bare bone rock. When he comes over the top of the first plateau, sweating and breathing heavily, the wind strikes him hard. From now on it will be twice the labour, climbing and bending into the wind.

Ocean before him, sky above it an unspoiled blue, though the land is still tamped down with cloud. He rests on a rock, folding to streamline himself in the wind. Turf-cutters have left here long strips of scarring. A nearby ram pauses to look at him, horns ingrown and curling to cage its skull. He thinks again about Ita's ironic hectoring when he turned up in the middle of the night without that Canadian lad. She woke when he was climbing into bed, asked where the boy was, then bashed him around with her pillow for his thoughtlessness. She harped for days.

The wind puts him on his feet. He climbs to the next plateau, the one before the summit, cliffs two thousand feet above the ocean. And now, staring over the grey sea, a mirror of his own foaming agitation, he hears the smash of breakers on the rocks below. The sound is like the Old Man's drum. The priest's words at the funeral: every one of us shall give account of himself to God. This is what has been waking him, shivering and nauseous, all along. Why at dawn he finds himself on the beach staring back at where he came from. One way or another, in this world or the next, sooner or later, truth will out.

For fourteen years, when he has thought of his other wife, she has been lying on her back in bed, mound of pregnant belly pushing up under the covers. Fourteen years later, she is sleeping still. She has not even rolled over. The fetus, arrested in the womb, floats patiently in its liquid world. All is as he left it the morning he emptied her purse and, walking out in the sunshine, broke with Canada. The blows he inflicted, her cries. The ocean and a gull wheeling below the cliff. She never told him no. Never said, 'Martin! Stop!' It made him crazy, her passivity. Meaner, his own shame. When he first came to Ireland, he saw a hag in a church yard. He felt her, even at a distance, searching his soul. She spat at him and this was joy – to know he could be resisted and saved from himself. Then he met Ita. He has been loved better than Ita loves him, even excepting her animal ways, but he has never loved more himself. He has been employed by love.

Above the nearly vertical cliff, the air is condensing on the green peak. It clots, whitens, swells, then is released to cloud over the land. And now, having reached the secret place where clouds are born, he is reminded of another birth. The image he saw at the funeral, his brother as a child, was the image of his own son.

He turns to the ocean. For a long time he stands leaning into the wind, watching the wavering line of horizon. As he stares, his eyes dry and tire and when he finally sees what he has come to see, he cannot be sure that such straining outward has not turned his vision back into himself. Far out in the Atlantic a dark bubble appears. It vanishes easily enough, only a pin-head at this distance. When it surfaces again it is larger, swollen, a blister on the water. He does not actually see it burst. Suddenly slick and black and glittering. It is spreading, moving toward shore, mourning, a funeral cortege. The stickiness of oil and dread.

Running down the mountain, not the way he came, down a spongy slope to the holy well. At the standing stone, he stumbles. Sacred carvings worn to pocked illegibility, he must touch to read. Fingers tremble over depressions, warnings, a child's face, a country. The well itself – a tiny spring trickling into a circle of stones, all around rusted offerings. He digs in his pocket, flings all the coins he has.

THE HYPOCHONDRIA CLUB

I
THE DIET DURING AND AFTER INFLUENZA
HORLICK'S MALTED MILK
VERY NUTRITIOUS, DIGESTIBLE
THE OLD RELIABLE ROUND PACKAGE

IN 1914, the day Claire came to work as a maid in the hotel, she walked up the stone steps to the front door like a paying guest. After that she would always be obliged to use the back entrance even when she was out of uniform. On the landing she met the doorman, his blue gaze fixed straight ahead, the polished buttons on his jacket so brassy they lured the crows. He was absolutely motionless until he swung open the door. Then her feet landed in the garden of the lobby carpet and the chandelier hung above her like seven moons. On the threshold of her new life she paused and looked back. Through the door panes the doorman seemed a beautiful statue, not a living man, and for a moment she so believed he was cast in some inanimate material that she unabashedly went for another look. He *was* alive! In an elegant sweep he opened the door again, ushering her back out on the landing.

'Do you dance?' he asked.

For an expert in motionlessness Andy proved to be an astonishingly good dancer. He two-stepped her over the par-quet of the Alexandria Club, spelling out private messages with his feet. BE MINE. YOU'RE SWEET. When he had danced her through the heels of all her silk stockings they got mar-ried.

They moved to a cottage near the hotel, living in a way that belied their employment: Claire hardly ever changed the sheets and Andy purposely left the door ajar. Neighbourhood cats broke from their nocturnal rounds to creep into bed with them. Waking in the night to the sound of purring, Claire would rub her face all over Andy. Of course she'd been a virgin bride, but Andy loved her like he danced with her; with him she could perform quite effortlessly steps she'd never danced before.

Yet any man able to stand unflinching for ten hours was already half a soldier. The morning Andy's company was leaving Victoria, Claire, packing for him, reached into the dresser. With a cry she drew back her hand. From Andy's dampened undershirts a tabby stared back at her, writhing with kittens. The night before, saying goodbye with their bodies, she and Andy had closed the perfect circle of ecstasy, brought the two ends together: pleasure and pleasure. In the same room at the same time the cat had been labouring through the agony of parturition.

'Don't worry, Claire, my darling Claire,' Andy told her as she wept. He kissed her hand where the cat had bitten it, held it, pressed her waist. The name of this waltz: 'Tenderness'. He spun her once around. 'I'll be home in a couple months. We'll have a litter of our own.'

After he was gone she didn't know what to do with all her desire. Then Peggy brought her to John's room to show she had not been exaggerating the contents of his medicine chest: Beecham's Pills, Oxygenos Tablets, Nuxated Iron, Bitro-Phosphate, Cod Liver Oil, Dr. Chase's Menthol Bags, Horlick's Malted Milk, Danderine, DDD Liquid Wash ... an arsenal of penny cures, a hypochondria museum. But what struck Claire was the variety of containers. She imagined opening each tin, jar, box, and bottle and storing there a tiny portion of her physical need for Andy to be uncapped later in doses more bearable. In the green jar she would put her longing for him to scratch her. The clear bottle for the way he had licked her like a cat.

They wrote often. In one letter from London Andy described a dance Claire had never heard of – the tango. He would bring her home the steps like a living souvenir. By then she had moved back to the hotel and installed herself with Peggy in the tiny staff quarters. She and Andy had conceived a child. If Housekeeping found out, she would be dismissed, so she told no one, not Peggy, not even Andy who had enough to worry about waterproofing his boots for the trenches.

Three months later she felt bloated with anxiety. Certain she was already showing, she asked if Peggy had noticed she was plumper.

'You?' laughed Peggy, who really was plump. 'Actually, you look wasted.'

In the linen room one morning Claire was reaching for a stack of towels on a high shelf, arms in the air when the first cramp gripped her. She dropped the towels and pressed her hands to her belly. Crouching to pick them up again, she saw they had landed in her blood.

II

A NEW BLOOD-FOOD HAS BEEN DISCOVERED
WORKS WONDERS
PUTS NEW LIFE INTO PEOPLE
FERROZONE TABLETS – CHOCOLATE COATED
TWO AFTER EVERY MEAL

PEGGY HELD UP a tin of Danderine. 'Dandruff will get every hair on your head! Let Danderine check nasty scurf and stop hair falling out!'

'Where did you get that?' asked Claire.

'From my Romeo, my Don John.'

'You snitched it.'

'I wanted a lock of his hair. He wouldn't give me one. I took this instead.' She set the tin in the very centre of the table and sat down across from Claire. 'Watch close,' she said. Head propped up on her elbows, fingers to her temples, she clenched her eyes and strained a fever-red. A minute later she exhaled with explosive relief.

'Did it move?'

'What?'

'The Danderine!'

In *The Daily Colonist* Spiritualists were writing letters to the editor, citing cases of telekinesis, raps, and levitations, proof that life is continuous after bodily death. 'While going about my household chores, I felt impressed upon by an invisible force. I felt hands lay upon mine and immediately I fell into a trance...' Peggy had read this aloud to Claire that morning, adding that she wished she would fall into a trance while a discarnate intelligence cleaned the hotel. Another writer testified to hearing 'Rule Britannia' rapped out at a séance, to luminous appearances and curtains swaying in draught-free rooms. It was the fall of 1918 and Andy lay in an unmarked grave in France. Supposedly the war was going to end.

'Do you believe in that?' asked Claire, pointing to the Danderine.

'I do. John used to have awful dandruff.'

It was for a lark then that they went together to the Open Door Spiritualist Church. Peggy couldn't decide what to wear. She thought black appropriate for a religion that seemed one long funeral. Claire said she had it backward: Spiritualists denied the very existence of death. In the end Peggy chose a sunny plaid, Claire a green wool skirt and bolero.

The church itself was an unremarkable wooden structure, formerly housing some staider sect. Arriving just as the service began, they were lucky to squeeze into a crowded pew together. The usual hymns: 'Nearer my God to Thee, Nearer to THEE!!' Cawing, Peggy glanced sidelong at Claire who had to bite her lip to keep from laughing. Then, from a door behind the flower-bedecked pulpit, the minister appeared, a tiny woman in an ordinary blue dress, grey hair scooped up in a bun – the Reverend Mrs Charles Abrams.

'Friends, there are two worlds,' said the Reverend Mrs Charles Abrams, her voice a contradiction of her stature. 'The world we presently know and the other. Between these worlds is a door that opens and closes, a door through which the spirit may come and go. Friends, we are standing before that door at this very moment. We are on the Threshold of the Unseen.'

After the sermon, while the collection plates were being circulated, Mrs Abrams came out from behind the pulpit and stood in the aisle with closed eyes. Claire watched her for a minute, then leaned into Peggy. 'A trance?'

Peggy rolled back her eyes, flashing whites.

They stifled their laughter behind handkerchiefs. Soon, though, the congregation resettled. When the room was completely silent Mrs Abrams came alive again, turning to a woman in the first pew. 'Annie, it's Philip. He says let Mother keep the medal. It would mean so much to her.'

Claire saw that Annie, who had leaned forward eagerly to receive her message, now fell back in a pique. She pulled a handkerchief out of her sleeve and pressed it to her eyes. Mrs Abrams then moved on to an elderly gentleman she evidently did not know and was asking if a blond child had any significance for him. 'That's our Edward!' he cried. Suddenly Claire recognized how truly she belonged in this congregation. The pews were filled with war widows like herself and mourning sweethearts and parents stopped by grief, people who, like Claire, were not really living.

Now Mrs Abrams was at the end of the aisle, looking directly at her. In the pulpit she had seemed old, but here was a glowing face reminiscent of the ones Claire had seen on devotional postcards and advertisements for restorative tonics. The eternal life Mrs Abrams promised was streaming off her.

'Madam, do you understand the name Andrew?'

Peggy gasped and clutched Claire's hand. Claire nodded.

'He wants you to know he's sorry about the kittens.'

Two years before, when she received the telegram announcing Andy's death, Claire had buried her wedding ring in the rose garden of the hotel. That was his funeral. And although she'd accepted the sympathy and condolences offered to her, she hadn't really grieved. 'Till death do us part' didn't seem to fit her situation. By then Andy had been away for twice the time she'd known him. She was more married to her yearning than to him. Now he would be *forever* overseas, she *forever* suspended in her waiting, but apart from *forever* nothing had really changed. This should have been something Mrs Abrams could respect – that yearning is as unsubject to distance and time and death as is a spirit. Instead she was telling Claire that from the moment the piece of shrapnel had opened a big red door in Andy's chest, he'd been there beside her, these two years.

Going about her work in the hotel the next day and the weeks that followed, she expected Andy in every bed she stripped. She pictured him reclining on one hip and smiling slyly, tracing his finger around the flower-shaped stain of someone else's lovemaking on the sheet. But she never did see him or even sense his presence, despite what Mrs Abrams had said. Mrs Abrams, she decided, was the kind of person who might taunt the blind by saying, 'Look!'

At night, to crowd out what she could not feel – Andy unembodied – she and Peggy slept together in Peggy's cot. Peggy snored fitfully and tossed. Claire lay fretting. Night was her time to mourn the baby she had lost. If it had survived, it would have been half Andy, would have kept him half alive. Lately she had been plagued by a spectral kicking in her belly. She imagined she was carrying a phantom foetus that would grow to term, then in agony be delivered – only to haunt her.

'Claire, I'm half dead! I need my sleep!' Peggy pleaded and this way persuaded her to see Mrs Abrams again. The war had ended, but on everybody's lips was a cruel rhyme: 'There was a little bird. It's name was Enza. I opened the window and in-flu-Enza...' Sneezing in public was banned, as were gatherings and church services. One evening in late November Claire, Peggy and John arrived for a private sitting.

Mrs Abrams lived across from a firehall that had been converted into an infirmary. 'All day I watch them run in with their milk puddings and their medicines, holding the spirit against its will in the body.' Eerie in the dusk, the firehall's lookout did seem a prison tower. Then Mrs Abrams, shaking her head in sorrowful incomprehension, ushered them into the house. She disposed of their wet overcoats and shoes and led them through to a parlour where the carpet had been rolled back and the drapes closed. Motioning for them to seat themselves at the table, she crossed to the fireplace to light the oil lamps that stood on either end of the mantel. When she switched off the electric light the red glass chimneys of the lamps cast the room in a strange wine-coloured glow. Mrs Abrams took her seat. ' "So-and-so is dead," they say. They don't understand how truly alive he's become.'

Claire began to cry. She bowed over the table and sobbed into her hands.

'See?' said Mrs Abrams. 'Needless sorrow.'

'Andy's alive?' said Claire, straightening in anger. 'Where is he then?'

Mrs Abrams did not reply, but instead offered Claire her outstretched hand. Peggy took the other. John was still wearing gloves.

'Please, sir. You must remove them.'

'And risk contracting influenza? Perhaps you might assure us of your credentials first.'

He looked as blanched as a cadaver, and as thin. Mrs Abrams burst out laughing. 'I am clairvoyant! You doubt me? Why? Infants are as perceptive. So are cats.'

Peggy kicked John under the table. With a show of indignation, he took off his gloves.

'I remind you, friends,' said Mrs Abrams when all their hands were linked, 'this circle is religious. Levity is not permitted.' She winked. 'Only levitation.'

They sang 'Jerusalem', then Mrs Abrams explained she would undress her psyche and don the pure raiment of a trance. John sniffed. Mrs Abrams closed her eyes. In ten minutes the room had chilled considerably and Mrs Abrams's hand in Claire's grew rigid and clammy. Then Claire instinctively understood what Spiritualists meant by a Presence. Strange, she realized she had known it all along. She recalled from childhood being alone and preoccupied in play, then sensing physically that she was being watched – that she was the focus of a benign and palpable gaze. It had happened countless times; when she looked up, expecting to see a parent, she saw no one.

Mrs Abrams said the letter 'A'. A knock sounded sharply on the table.

'Oh, my God.' John attempted to free his hands, but they were fused with Peggy's and Claire's. He could only raise their side of the circle. Reciting the alphabet again, Mrs Abrams's voice was oddly devoid of modulation. On 'N', the same knock sounded, though no one had contact with the table.

'Andy?' said Claire.

'One rap means no. Three raps mean yes,' said Mrs Abrams in monotone. 'Are we in the presence of Andy?'

A short volley of knocks. Claire once more began to sob.

'Tell her to get over it!' Peggy said. 'Andy, will you tell her?'

'Are you happy?' cried John.

Through the sickening long silence they waited for an answer. When it finally came, a single penetrating rap, it was a sound more hopeless than the telegram-bearing messenger's knuckles on the door, worse than the dawn's first shot, a hollow echo over muddy trenches. One rap means no: *the living were never to be released from suffering.* No: *neither the dead.*

Across the room, a second rap, two more in quick succession on the table, another on the ceiling. From all around the room, the furniture, walls and floor, on every surface graced with the gift of resonance, a rhythm was rapped out. Slow, slow, quick-quick, slow. Slow, slow, quick-quick, slow. In confusion they looked to Mrs Abrams; on her face, a blissful smile.

III
TO BUILD UP YOUR HEALTH
COD LIVER OIL WITH HYPOPHOSPHITES
MALT EXTRACT AND WILD CHERRY
NO TASTE OF OIL – PLEASANT TO TAKE.
THE BEST RECONSTRUCTIVE TONIC.

ONE OF THE MAIDS, while changing the linen in a third floor room, threw back the bedspread to reveal a new-born babe abandoned in crumpled blood-soaked sheets. It was alive, so she set it on her trolley while she remade the bed – perfect pleated corners – then wheeled it to Housekeeping and turned it in as she would a cigarette case or a pair of gloves inadvertently left behind.

Claire didn't believe the story. Before the war a different rumour used to circulate: an animal, usually a cougar, made its predatory way from the wooded outskirts of the city to the hotel where it mauled to death an American guest. But by

1919 death no longer made the heart thrill. Life did.

Another change since the war was how any male guest in full possession of health and limb would receive appraising glances from the maids. Mr Stowe, though decidedly not handsome, possessed at least those merits. He'd also arrived in January with a brilliant tan, so was turning heads phototropically. Further to his credit was his enigmatic vocation, the source of much romantic speculation. Peggy, who had searched his room while cleaning it, declared him a museum man. In the bottom of the bureau, tucked among his underdrawers: a thick white bone tapered to a wedge, a carved stick decorated with black feathers, enormous beetles pressed into stones.

Surprisingly, none of the younger maids seemed to appeal to him, despite their coyness, the way, for example, they tickled the furniture with their feather dusters. He fixed instead on Claire, which annoyed as much as flattered her. He tagged her through the corridors, obstructed the passage of her trolley, stalled her with clumsy dialogue. 'Tell me ... ah ... is it true about this baby?'

Guests had been pestering her all day about the baby and she was weary of it. In mock distress she patted the sheets and towels stacked on her trolley. 'Oh, dear! I had one here myself, but it must have rolled off!'

Mr Stowe stood there blinking. Claire pushed her trolley on to the next room and was fishing in her apron pocket for the key. Mr Stowe caught up. 'Ah... Our lads will be home next week.'

'Yes, sir, they will.' She unlocked the door.

'You're looking especially forward to it, I would imagine.'

'We all are, sir.'

'I mean ... ah ...'

She wheeled the trolley into the room.

'Surely some lad will be coming home to claim you!'

'Andy was killed, sir,' Claire said and made to close the door behind her. Mr Stowe stopped it with his foot.

'My God! How thoughtless! Forgive me!'

'It's quite all right,' said Claire – sincerely. Although she was not exactly a convert to Spiritualism, the sitting with Mrs Abrams two months before had worked in her some kind of cure. The very night of the séance she had braved her cot alone, lay waiting for Peggy's first spasmodic snore. Then, mouthing the alphabet, she quietly tapped out Andy's name upon the wall. Summonsed, he appeared, or rather the way he used to make her feel appeared, sliding under the sheets with her. Disadvantaged by intangibility, he took loan of her hands and raised her nightgown to her neck. Then he touched her in the old way so when she came to gasp out loud she knew it was Andy's love that had moved her. Afterward she slept so deeply she could not remember in the morning his tingling departure, the drawing out of his spirit from her body.

Mr Stowe was begging, 'Let me make it up to you!'

'Really, that's not necessary.'

'Yes! Yes! I insist!' He scratched his moustache with agitation, then offered her his peace. 'Do you know the tango?'

'I've heard of it. It's a dance.'

IV
NUXATED IRON
NUXATED IRON HELPS PUT
ASTONISHING STRENGTH AND ENERGY
INTO THE VEINS OF MEN AND BRING ROSES
TO THE CHEEKS OF PALE, NERVOUS,
RUN-DOWN WOMEN.

THEY USED TO roll bandages for the war effort in the cafeteria of the hotel. Now Peggy stood in the middle of their little room holding her elbows out and the tail of a left-over bandage in her corset. Slowly Claire circled her, binding her breasts flat to her ribs.

'Can you breathe?' asked Claire.

'Never mind about breathing.'

Claire tucked the loose end in the corset, then brought Peggy her shapeless frock. Peggy pulled it over her head and moved her bulk stiffly to the mirror. She frowned. 'It doesn't matter what I look like anyway.' She eased onto the chair, opened her compact and began to batter her face with powder.

'You look lovely,' said Claire.

In the mirror, Peggy feigned vomiting.

They were going to sneak down to Mr Stowe's room and learn how to dance the tango. He had initially asked Claire to meet him in the Palm Court, but when she explained that fraternizing with guests was forbidden, he suggested instead a clandestine gathering of a few friends in his room. Now Peggy was afraid John would beg off again. The longer she courted him, the less carnal he became. Last week they went to the pictures: *Kaiser, Beast of Berlin.* 'The Kaiser is a slave to beautiful hands!' She'd removed her glove and dropped her own plump hand in his lap; through the whole picture he managed staunchly to ignore it. At thirty-one, she wished she'd been lucky enough to have a husband killed in the war.

Peggy improved her eyebrows then, taking up a pot of rouge, rubbed two pink blossoms on her cheeks. Around the edge of the mirror, a fringe of patent medicine advertisements she'd cut out of *The Daily Colonist.* As her own remedy for frustration she would occasionally unstick one, 'Hamilton's Pills cleanse the liver and move the bowels while you sleep...', put it in an envelope and post it anonymously to John.

In the mirror: Claire sitting on the end of her cot smoking pensively, blond hair crimped around her head, voguishly flat-chested in her black dress. Peggy was glad her pretty friend had such a promising suitor. Earlier that day she'd even told Claire, 'This is your chance to get out of the linen cupboard!' At the same time, she wanted to rail against her own disadvantage, which was that her beautiful spirit was misrepresented by her body. She hated, too, how Claire so perfectly belonged in hers.

Once Peggy had been kissed. She and a schoolfriend balancing in a tree, their curiosity mutual. When they pressed lips, Peggy opened hers slightly to feel the kiss on the slippery part of her mouth. Her friend dropped off the branch like a ripened fruit, landed splat on her feet, then fled shrieking across the field. They never spoke again. Sometimes Peggy touched her own breasts, but wouldn't put her hand near her privates because, long ago, her mother had warned her that the smell would never come off her fingers.

The Daily Colonist reported that thirty thousand Canadians had so far died of Spanish influenza. Peggy longed to catch a different disease. Whenever possible, she exposed herself to its contagion. She searched out the infected, usually other maids, but sometimes even women she didn't know – in shops or the streetcar – women who wore the fevered glow of desire. Then she'd knock against them and in the flurry of mutual apologies, whisk a handkerchief out of a cuff or pocket. Later she'd hold it over her nose and mouth, breathing through it, like the masks people wore to *prevent* influenza. Claire, too, had the malady, had suffered it for years. Every morning Peggy let her go ahead to the cafeteria, then exchanged their pillow slips. All in vain; Peggy, it seemed, was immune.

She looked again at Claire. Cigarette finished, she was lying back on the cot. 'One rap means no,' said Peggy. 'Three raps mean yes.'

Claire smiled.

'Is it wonderful?'

Raising her arm languidly, Claire knocked three times on the wall.

'Better than food?'

Laughing, she knocked three times again.

'Would you marry for it?'

Claire rolled over and gaped at Peggy. 'John's finally asked you?'

'Don John?' Peggy brought her knuckles down hard on the dresser. 'I think I'll die if I don't find out soon! Is it worse for you, knowing what it's like?'

Three raps. John was knocking at the door.

V
TO AROUSE A SLUGGISH LIVER, TO RELIEVE A DISTRESSED STOMACH, TO FORTIFY YOURSELF AGAINST DISEASE – USE BEECHAM'S PILLS

THE FURNITURE had been pushed back, a fire lit. By the window – a gramophone, its bell like morning glory. Mr Stowe greeted them with a bottle of prohibited champagne swaddled in a towel like a baby. 'For medicinal purposes,' he jested, inviting them into the room. By the fireplace, he poured them each a glass. The next day the *Empress of Asia* would be docking, bringing Victoria's first soldiers home from Europe. The mayor had declared a civic holiday; even the maids and men like John, who sorted the soiled linen in the hotel basement, would be let off. They raised their glasses in a unanimous toast to the occasion.

Claire asked, 'Where did you learn the tango, Mr Stowe?'

'In London, on my way back from Egypt. It's been the rage there since before the war.'

'Egypt!' Peggy exclaimed. 'That's where you got your tan! Most of the girls guessed Bermuda!'

He blushed.

'What were you doing in Egypt?' asked Claire.

'Ah... Nothing really. I'm just a hobby traveller with a penchant for bizarre souvenirs.' He set his glass on the mantel. 'Shall we walk through it first without the music?'

John turned to Peggy in alarm. She followed him into a corner – the closest he had let her come in months. 'Do I take it we're dancing?' he hissed.

She fixed on him a pout.

'This ... this is how influenza is transmitted!'

'Thin people should take Bitro-Phosphate to put on firm and healthy flesh!' The words flew off her tongue before she even thought them. She clapped her hand over her mouth.

John recoiled. 'You! *You're* the one!'

'One what?' But already he had wheeled around and was heading for the door. She scurried after him and snagged him by the sleeve. 'Please, stay. Please.' He really did look ill – waxy and shaken.

'Have you been tormenting me through the mail?'

'I don't know what you're talking about!'

Then he cast down his eyes and she knew he believed her. 'My stomach...' he muttered, sniffing.

'Poor thing.' Patting his arm, she gently manoeuvred him about-face. 'It's not ... gas?'

'No, no.'

'Nerves.' And somehow she had guided him back to the fireplace where Claire and Mr Stowe were exchanging awkward commentaries in an attempt not to overhear. More champagne was offered. They drank a moment in silence, then Mr Stowe cleared his throat and strode into the middle of the carpet.

'The gentleman extends his right hand. The lady, ah ... if she so desires ... accepts the dance by pressing her palm to his.' These instructions he addressed to John. Then he turned and boldly looked at Claire.

She had not tasted alcohol since before the war, had never tried champagne. Mr Stowe, suddenly confident and chivalrous, almost handsome in his dapper suit, was waiting with his arm stretched out to her. She came forward, pressed her palm to his, then drew back for a second, the gesture reminding her of the time she'd been bitten by a cat.

'The gentleman takes the lady securely in his arms.' He gripped Claire's waist and pulled her to him.

Peggy gripped John's waist and pulled him to her.

'No, no!' cried Mr Stowe. 'The gentleman always leads.' He let go of Claire and went to help the confused couple reverse positions. Standing there, Claire realized it was the first time in years a man had touched her. He had drawn her body to his, then let go, yet the ghost of the sensation remained on her hands and waist. She was trying to decide which she preferred, the actual touch or the sweetness of having been touched, when Mr Stowe took her in his arms again.

'The basic tango steps are "the walk" and "the close". "The walk" you've known since age two. Gentlemen go forward, ladies back. "The close" – Let me show you.'

A *living* man had his arms around her. She'd forgotten how much heat came off a body, how moist skin was. He commandeered her two steps back. 'Watch now! Tang-o close!' Without conscious effort, she danced the step with him.

'We'll do that again. Follow us, if you will.'

John refused to move. He wrested his hands away from Peggy and wiped them peevishly across his jacket front.

Mr Stowe cleared his throat. 'Perhaps ... ah ... more champagne?'

As he refilled their glasses, Peggy, red-faced, headed for the lavatory. Claire followed, found her with her dress thrown over her face, clawing at the bandage round her chest. 'Undo me,' she croaked from under her crepy tent. 'I'm dying.'

Claire tugged loose the tail of the bandage and began unravelling. 'Why don't you dance with Mr Stowe?'

'He wants to dance with you.'

'We'll take turns.'

'I think I'll go.'

'You can't!' cried Claire.

The bandage fell in a loop at Peggy's feet. She tore the dress off her face, inhaled and exhaled in a gust. She peered in the mirror. 'You are so beautiful,' she told her puffy, over-made reflection. 'I *love* you.'

Claire stayed behind, rolled up the bandage and stashed it behind the toilet. Back in the other room Peggy was already chattering gaily with Mr Stowe. 'On Monday night at the Hypochondria Club, there's a veterans' dance!'

'Where?'

She giggled. 'The *Alexandria* Club.'

'Splendid!' said Mr Stowe. 'We'll all go and introduce the tango. You ladies will make the society page.'

Peggy sighed, glancing at John humped like a vulture on the sofa. Seeing Claire, Mr Stowe quickly drained his glass. He held his hands out to her, then led her back out on the carpet.

He reviewed the steps they had already learned, demonstrated briefly 'the promenade', then, without warning, lunged forward, dipping Claire and hovering over her, their bodies a double arc. Tilting back her head, Claire felt his breath on her throat, imagined how solid he would feel on top of her. Something she missed – the sensation of weightfulness. Then she was certain of her preference: to be manifestly touched.

'*That*,' said Mr Stowe, lifting Claire back on her feet, 'was "the corte".'

'Deadly,' muttered John. 'Absolutely deadly.'

'Shall we try now with the music?'

He crossed to the gramophone. 'Listen to the rhythm. This is what makes the tango unmistakable.' He put the needle down. After an initial pop, the orchestra responded. Piano, violin, the sighing of a concertina, then a melancholy baritone, his voice a panacea. A few bars into the song and Claire stood rapt. It had nothing to do with the lyrics, which she could not understand, but the rhythm, a heart skipping beats, anticipation.

'What's he singing?' asked Peggy.

'It's Spanish.' Mr Stowe cocked his ear. '*Saquen ustedes sus pañuelos*. Take out your ... handkerchiefs? *Mi gran amor esta muerta*. My true love is ... ?'

'Why?' asked John suddenly. 'Why do they call it *Spanish* influenza?'

'Let me tap the rhythm out for you.' Mr Stowe rapped his knuckles against the fireplace mantel. 'Slow, slow, quick-quick, slow.'

Claire started violently. 'Oh, God!' cried John, as Peggy sank down next to him on the sofa. From his nose, a sudden sluice of blood.

VI
THIN, NERVOUS PEOPLE NEED BITRO-PHOSPHATE

JOHN SAT on the edge of the bath staunching his nosebleed with a towel, pondering what he knew of spirit rapping. In volume it ranged from the lightest tap to what could be likened to a sledge-hammer blow. It imitated horses trotting, bouncing balls, the striking of a match, *even the rhythms of popular tunes and dances*. Mrs Abrams's own husband, long since passed into the Unseen, had a habit of sounding footsteps a few paces behind her almost everywhere she went. He had learned so much from Mrs Abrams: how the variety of spirit rapping is infinite; how life is infinite.

He peered cautiously into the towel. The bleeding finally stopped, he folded under the stain, laid the towel in the bath, then stood to inspect his nostrils in the mirror. His complexion was porridgy and anaemic. He would go to his room at once and take two Ferrozone tablets.

Instead he sank down again, pressed his knuckles to his mouth, a stopper against his advancing sob. He usually felt like this in the morning before descending to the mildewed and miasmic basement of the hotel, the heaps of soiled linen. The men he worked with bullied and derided him. What had kept them back from war: age, lameness, a glass marble for an eye. John's trivial ailments insulted them. They balled up towels and pelted him until he was completely buried. Yesterday they bound him up in a sheet like a mummy.

When finally able to take his hand from his mouth, he sat for a long time staring at it. Like the other, and his feet, it was chapped raw and scaled with eczema. Then there was his private affliction: an undescended testicle which, he was convinced, affected his gait so that his right knee throbbed ceaselessly. And despite the grandiose claims of the Hamilton Pill Company, *he got no relief*. Why stay alive? Life was unremedied suffering. Death, if he understood correctly, was just the passing through a doorway to a better life. He was even acquainted with Andy the doorman, had heard him testify percussively to his happiness: slow, slow, quick-quick, slow. Yet John lacked the will to open even the lavatory door.

Three raps. He stood up in alarm.

Peggy pushed her face in. 'Are you all right?'

'No,' said John. 'I feel awful.'

She rolled her eyes. 'Come out and have a cup of tea.'

'That was Andy's tune, wasn't it?'

She looked away. Then he knew: even the undaunted Peggy was spooked.

VII
WE ARE PROMPT.
WE ARE CAREFUL.
FOR DISINFECTING AND PURIFYING YOUR HOME
OXYGENOS

'THESE PAST four years I have been on a kind of pilgrimage.

You see ... ah ... I successfully avoided the ladies of the "Knit or Fight" campaign. Then I escaped the age of conscription by just three days. Our present epidemic has not touched me either. In fact, I haven't sneezed in four years.'

Evidently Mr Stowe felt responsible for the strained silence, felt, as host, he should press on with talk. He settled on the sofa next to Claire and Peggy.

'I guess we're done then with the tango,' he said.

No one responded. John hunched deeper in the armchair. Only good manners kept them on his furniture, distracted, glancing at one another. Mr Stowe cleared his throat again.

'I told you I have a penchant for souvenirs. In truth, I've been collecting what one might call "death trinkets". I went to the Badlands for fossils and to Mexico where I bought a celebrated shroud. In my possession – over two hundred charms and amulets and a human skull.'

Claire shivered. 'You have morbid taste, Mr Stowe!'

'Don't think that I love these things! They disgust me!'

'Then why do you collect them?'

He seemed embarrassed by his own answer. 'You'll say I'm superstitious. I have doted on death. I have bought it presents, flattered it, and this way avoided it. My collection? I owe it my life.'

A confession foisted upon strangers. They looked away. John made a discordant bell stirring his tea with his spoon. Then it was Peggy who could not bear the awkward silence. 'Tell us about Egypt, Mr Stowe.'

'I went to see the tombs and to learn more about the ancient Egyptian cult of death. They believed that the soul and the spirit – the "Ba" and the "Ka" – were immortal, *physically* immortal. If the body were properly preserved, the "Ka" would return to enjoy the benefits of life: eating, playing cards,' he chuckled nervously, 'dancing the tango ...'

Claire started, clattering her cup and saucer.

'May I ... ah ... tell you a story?' He turned to Claire for consent but did not or would not see the contradiction in her polite nod.

'A bazaar in Cairo. A hellish place swarming with flies and

hashish cases and street urchins clawing at my pockets. I was looking for scarabs – '

'What are scarabs?' asked Peggy.

John grimaced. 'Sounds like a disease.'

'An amulet shaped like a beetle, commonly tucked in a mummy's wrappings. Anyway, most of what I found there was fake or ridiculously dear, so I headed back to the hotel, stopping on the way to buy an orange. I wanted to avoid the beggars. There was a track running between that fruit stall and the next, so I followed it, ended up in an alley and stood there peeling my orange in peace.'

Now he had their full attention. He paused to sip his tea.

'I had eaten about half of it, when I heard a peculiar sound ... I understate. It was a cry.'

'What kind of cry?' asked Peggy.

'To tell the truth, I thought it was a baby. My sister's child used to shriek like that. Blood-thinning. Gave me the shivers. I wanted to run, but it occurred to me that the infant might be unattended and in danger. What I could have done about it, I don't know.' He smiled and shrugged. 'I've never held a baby in my life!'

'But it wasn't a baby!' John blurted.

'It certainly wasn't, but I didn't know it then. Like the fool who fancies himself a hero, I hastened down the alley until I came to a grove of trees. I walked straight into it and for a minute was blinded while my eyes adjusted to the dimness. Suddenly I found myself standing in a throng of the most emaciated, scabious, flea-devoured cats I have ever seen. There must have been a hundred of them, earless, tailless, bald, rubbing up against me! Ach! The fleas! The place was zinging with fleas!'

Peggy and Claire cringed. Shuddering, John put his face in his hands.

'Naturally I fled. I tore down the alley and landed back in the bazaar face to face with an American. He was obviously a hashish addict; he had that queer glazed look. "Friend", he said, "I'm short on funds. Want to buy a mummified cat?"'

They gaped at him.

'It's true, I swear! He had it with him in a bag. I looked at it and, to my surprise, saw it was genuine. You can imagine how, after what had just occurred, it seemed like revenge, not to mention how invaluable it would be in my collection.'

'You bought it?' asked Peggy.

'How could I not? I have it here. Would you like to see it?'

Without waiting for an answer, he got up and crossed to the wardrobe, brought back an oblong package tied up in brown paper. He placed it on the table in front of Claire.

'Why would they make a mummy of a cat?' asked Claire.

'They worshipped cats. The goddess Bast was part woman and part cat.' He handed her a letter opener. She stared down at the package.

'Go on,' said Peggy.

Claire cut the string and carefully unfolded the paper. A bundle of brittle faded reeds bound together at both ends by crude cords. A girdle of roughly stitched linen.

'Oh,' said Peggy, disappointed. 'That's not what I expected.'

'Nor I,' said Claire, relieved.

Mr Stowe seemed miffed. 'It's over three thousand years old. I was tremendously lucky to get it. I paid dearly.'

'How exactly do they make a mummy?' asked John.

'They take its brains out through its nose...'

John recoiled. He drew his handkerchief from his jacket and daubed at his nostrils.

'... disembowel it, soak it in briny water, wrap it up...'

Enumerating these macabre instructions, he kept one eye on Claire. It unnerved her. What she had begun to realize with his earlier confession: Mr Stowe was not shy, as she had originally thought. He was peculiar. Abruptly she stood up.

'... vital organs in special urns – ' Mr Stowe halted in mid-explanation. 'You're not leaving!'

'I'm very tired. Thank you, Mr Stowe, for an extremely interesting evening.'

'You can't go. We... I...' He looked at the empty champagne bottle swaddled on the mantel, at the drained tea cups. Peggy and John rose as well. Mr Stowe blinked down at the mummy. 'I thought ... I thought we might ... ah ... unwrap the kitty.'

Peggy brightened. 'Oh! That would be fun!'

'You're not serious,' said Claire. 'You paid – '

'It would be worth it if you stayed.'

'You're going to open it?' asked John.

'Yes!' said Peggy. Seating herself again, she smiled goadingly at Claire.

'A dead animal? Expose it to the air? How unhygienic!'

Peggy said, 'Mr Stowe, we'll need scissors.'

He disappeared into the lavatory. Claire hissed at Peggy: 'I want to go!' but Mr Stowe was there again, scissors in hand, a tiny pair evidently for trimming his moustache. He passed them to Claire. She shot Peggy a furious look.

'Go on,' said Mr Stowe.

Claire took a breath and sat back down on the sofa. She hesitated a moment, then leaned over the mummy and began to cut away the strip of linen that bound the bundle in the middle. John maintained his distance, breathing through his handkerchief.

She unloosed the cord at one end, a knot tied three thousand years ago by hands that grieved a cat. The other cord disintegrated as she touched it, fibres crumbling into tiny bristles.

Mr Stowe moaned when he saw it.

Claire stopped. 'You don't want me to.'

'Oh, no. Do. Do.' He winced.

'You don't.'

'Yes!'

The desperation in his voice startled her. She turned back to the mummy and wriggled one of the reeds gingerly. Even with the bindings gone, they held fast together. Centuries had cemented them. With a dry snap it broke off, releasing a burst of scent: dust, spices. An insect tumbled out.

'Ah ha!' cried Mr Stowe. 'A genuine scarab.' He picked it up and showed the women its two mirrored wings. In his palm it crumbled to a powder.

Soon Claire had removed enough reeds to see the tea-brown wrappings of the mummy beneath it. Then Peggy joined in and a few minutes later the shrivelled form lay before them like a piece of swaddled driftwood.

'Meow,' said Peggy.

The first layer of cloth was a widely spaced strip holding in place a loose shroud. With the scissors, Claire cut the strip at the head. It crackled like strudel pastry as she unwound and dropped it in a crisp loop on the carpet. She slit the shroud down the middle. Underneath: tighter overlapping bindings, the tip of a curled dry paw poking out.

'You hold it and I'll unwind,' Peggy suggested.

This would be less awkward; she would not have to keep turning the mummy over. Cringing, Claire propped it upright in her lap. Peggy proved less careful with unravelling, tearing away the bindings in crusty segments. Hard nodes of insects, dirt, spilled into Claire's skirt.

'Here's the head now,' Peggy announced like a midwife.

Except for the very top of the head, most of the fur had rubbed away, exposing a luminous caramel scalp. Peggy peeled off another section. The cat's ears, too, had been completely abraded by the bindings. She slid her fingers under the next strip, pulled.

'Oh, God!' cried John.

Not the face of a cat, though Peggy continued tearing enthusiastically at the wrappings until two very human shoulders appeared. She drew back with a shriek.

The mummy baby gazed up at Claire from ancient desiccated sockets. Skin like leather, squashed face both old and young. Instinctively Claire loved its puckering mouth, drew it closer to her breast. Between the burnished lips she slipped her finger. Ageless hunger had preserved the moisture in the infant tongue. It slid wet over her finger and sucked.

VIII
THE GREAT SECRET OF KEEPING HEALTHY AND REGAINING HEALTH AFTER ILLNESS IS KEEPING THE BLOOD PURE, RICH AND RED. DR. CHASE'S NERVE FOOD STRENGTHENS THE ACTION OF THE HEART.

'PONDER THIS,' Mrs Abrams had said in her sermon. 'We are dead now. *This* is death, our unhappy days and nights. What we have been instructed to call dying – *that* is birth. How much sweeter to be unencumbered by the physical body, its weaknesses and ailments and desires. When a body dies, there should be great rejoicing. When a child is born, we ought to have a wake.'

In the lavatory Claire turned on the running water to pour over the sound of her weeping. For all perished children she cried, for their small places in the long history of sorrow, and her own child, whose life she had been unable to sustain in her body. Then she splashed herself with water knowing she would never wash away the stain of grief. The towel was lying in the bath. Picking it up to dry her face, she saw it was dyed with her own blood.

She had stayed a long time in the lavatory. When she came out the mummy baby was no longer on the table and she was alone with Mr Stowe.

'Where's Peggy?'

'She said she would wait for you in your room.' He advanced a step toward her. 'Please stay. I beg you. I've been waiting all night.'

He took her now as he would begin the tango and when she stepped back to escape him, made that part of the dance. Tang-o close. Corte. Their bodies hovered together. He set her back on her feet, then rolled her off his hip, promenaded her to the middle of the room. Corte. He pressed her mouth. She pushed him off. Mr Stowe seized her by the arm.

'I've never been in love. I've been right round the world, but never visited the heart. Would you call that a life?'

'Mr Stowe, that has nothing to do with me.'

'It does. Oh, yes it does.'

He gripped her tightly by the waist, dropping to his knees, and then through her skirt, cleaved her thighs with his face. Though she struck at him, he held on, nosing deeper, inhaling and forcing her off balance. She fell. Then he climbed atop of her and drew her dress over her hips. Now the strength behind each blow was the sudden sure conviction that Andy's spirit was not dead. Nor would it die, ever, while she allowed it to come to her and enjoy the benefits of life. When she was seemingly alone, Andy guided her in pleasure. Mr Stowe, his hand now tangled in her underdrawers, hurting and stabbing her, he had sensed it. In the persistence of desire – eternal life. He found the door in her body. Entering with his fingers, he reared up with a lonely groan. A wet stain spread across the unopened flies of his trousers. From exhaustion and pity she left off striking him. He panted like a dying man.

IX
TO AVOID THE 'FLU' RIDE A 'C.C.M.' BICYCLE.
GET AWAY FROM THE STUFFY CROWDS
AND THE DANGER OF CONTAGION.
RIDE A BICYCLE THROUGH THE PURE, FRESH AIR.

JOHN HAS NOT risen from his cot. He would not have witnessed anyway the joyous moment when the *Empress of Asia* docks; he does not circulate in crowds. Last night he took a Ferrozone tablet and two Beecham's Pills, but hardly slept at all. His throat feels packed with dust; his right knee throbs. Shivering, he rolls in the cot, but cannot rid himself of the eternal pitted stare of the mummy baby. When he touches his own crackling lips, he feels they are the colour of tobacco and three thousand years old.

A knock. A spirit knock or the work of living knuckles, he can no longer differentiate, nor does he care. He negotiates his legs over the edge of the cot, manages to sit up, but before he can summon further energy to stand, the door swings open. It's Andy, fresh off the *Empress of Asia*. He looks good: tall and rakish in his doorman's uniform – healthy. Andy strides forward and shakes John's hand. Clapping him on the back, he sends aching waves across John's body.

'Friend,' Andy says, 'your nose.'

Between John's feet: blood. Strange, each drop, as it hits the floor, reverberates like a sledge-hammer blow. Slam. Slam. Andy is laughing. Slam. A towel suddenly lands over John's head. He buries his face in it and sobs.

Andy sitting next to him on the cot, circling him in his arm.

'I'm ill,' John whimpers.

'You were ill last time I saw you.'

'What was wrong with me?'

'Piles!'

'I've still got piles.' He lifts his face from the bloody towel. 'Tell me...'

'Anything, friend.'

'Do you know the tango?'

Then Andy is prodding him gently to his feet, bracing a hand around his waist, John staggering more than standing. He clings to Andy's neck, bleeding on his shoulder. Two steps back. Andy rolls him off his hip. Dizzy, John has no focus, sees the room as a blur. 'Da, da, da-da, da!' Andy sings, beating out the rhythm with his heels. 'Da, da, da-da, da!' Promenade. Across the little room the door is open.

Down at the pier, Peggy squeals, bounces, waves her Union Jack ecstatically. Far out in the harbour the *Empress of Asia* is anchored for quarantine inspection. She can see each one of the two hundred and forty-three soldiers leaning over the ship's railing, waving back at her. The entire city has come down to welcome home the living. They overload the street-cars, crash through safety barriers, tote a thousand pies and cakes. On every masthead along the pier: a coloured flag. Boys on bicycles zip up and down Dallas Road, playing cards salvo in their spokes. Then a pipe band strikes up a Scottish tune and drowns out Peggy's cheering.

Wending her way now through the crowd, Peggy steps lively; so far she has pinched four handkerchiefs. At a welcome stand she stops to buy an apple which she hopes later to toss to a soldier coming down the gangplank. In her hand the red and shiny fruit reminds her of desire.

From the corner of her eye she sees him.

'Mr Stowe! Oh, Mr Stowe!'

She is sure he saw her too, but why would he about-face so hastily? She tails him through the throng, loses him, then stands on her tiptoes craning above the bobbing heads. The moment she gives up, she spots him – at a nearby booth where

Panama hats are being sold to honour the ship's route through the Canal. His back is to her as he makes his purchase. She sneaks up behind him and waits for him to turn.

'Boo!'

Mr Stowe colours deeply. She likes how he is flustered to see her. Holding her apple against his cheek, she teases. 'My, Mr Stowe, but you are red!'

He flaps the Panama hat, not meeting her eye. 'Ah...'

'Did you buy that?' asks Peggy, tugging on the hat brim. 'It doesn't seem your kind of souvenir.'

She steps back and tosses him the apple. Fumbling, he manages to catch it. He studies her a moment before breaking into a nervous smile. Then he pops the Panama hat over the crown of her hat. They both laugh.

'Mr Stowe, you didn't forget?' asks Peggy coyly.

'What?'

'The veterans' dance! Monday at the Hypochondria Club.'

'You haven't read the papers.' He polishes the apple on his lapel, then bites it. 'They've put a ban on dancing.'

'Oh, no!' Peggy cries. 'Not again!'

Claire only stays a moment on the crowded dock. It is too painful to see the men anchored so close, then enduring yet another separation. She wonders, in fact, why, having come this far, they don't leap over the ship's railings and swim. The woman in front of her, baby in her arms, can barely withstand the anticipation. She heaves volcanic sighs and mutters to herself. In a moment she will cry.

From over the mother's shoulder the baby blinks at Claire. Claire smiles and wiggles her fingers, sees the sweet face pucker with delight. 'Ba ba,' says the baby reaching out its little hand. Then the pipe band strikes the first long melancholy note of a Scottish ballad. Above their heads the gulls screech as dolefully. Ka! Ka! Ka! Claire turns and begins her walk back to the hotel.

She stands at the foot of the stone stairs. Today there is no one to prohibit her from entering through the front door, though neither is there a doorman to open it for her. She proceeds up the steps. On the landing she reaches for the brass handle, has barely touched it, when it swings open. In the empty lobby, under the chandelier's seven moons, she pauses a moment and looks back.

ACKNOWLEDGEMENTS

EIGHT OF THE stories in this collection were previously published in *Saturday Night*, *The Malahat Review*, *Quarry*, *Event*, *Canadian Fiction Magazine*, *Grain* and *Cyphers* (Dublin). 'The Chmarnyk', 'Shiners' and 'Oil and Dread' were reprinted in the Oberon Press anthology *Coming Attractions '92*. 'Oil and Dread' also appeared in the *Journey Prize Anthology 5*. The Coteau Books anthology *Out of Place* included 'And the Children Shall Rise'. 'The Chmarnyk' and 'The Hanging Gardens of Babylon' were both third prize winners in the 1988 and 1991 CBC Literary Competitions. 'The Chmarnyk' was also nominated for a 1993 National Magazine Award.